He wanted

But he knew he should ignore every feeling he had. Because he was going to get his heart smashed. Again. ...ext words proved it.

...know why I left, Cameron. Why I couldn't be ...ou then. You were getting serious and I couldn't ...down."

...ou left for New York and didn't look back?"

..." she replied. "And in two weeks I'll be going ...So, if anything happened it would—"

...on pushed off the counter. As he moved, the air ...l on some invisible axis. Hotter, thicker, as if a ...' something sinfully seductive had blown into ...m.

...ning is, Grace, if you want comfort—I can give ...at. If you want sex—I can give you that. But ...ow I'll still be me. And you'll still be the same ...ı who wanted to get away from here."

...oved closer. "Tomorrow isn't tonight. Make love ...'

# DATE WITH DESTINY

### BY
### HELEN LACEY

**Helen Lacey** grew up reading *Black Beauty, Anne of Green Gables* and *Little House on the Prairie*. These childhood classics inspired her to write her first book when she was seven years old, a story about a girl and her horse. She continued to write, with the dream of one day being a published author, and writing for Mills & Boon® Cherish™ is the realization of that dream. She loves creating stories about strong heroes with a soft heart and heroines who get their happily-ever-after. For more about Helen, visit her website, www.helenlacey.com.

For Gareth
1966–2009
Forever in my heart

## Chapter One

Grace Preston stared down at her bare feet peeking out from the hem of her long dress. Her sister's beach wedding had been romantic and casual—exactly what the bride and groom wanted. But it had left her without shoes and feeling more than a little exposed.

Grace didn't bother to pull up her dress as she walked toward the water's edge. To hell with it—she'd never wear the halter style blue-green chiffon concoction again anyway. The water was cold and she ignored the wet sand clinging to her heels. The moon hung low in the sky, casting a great sliver of light across the ocean. The sound of cresting waves was faintly hypnotic and she relaxed a bit, taking a long swallow from the champagne flute in her hand. Once the glass was empty she quickly refilled it from the bottle she held in the other.

It wasn't like she intended to get drunk. That wasn't her

style. She simply needed to be alone. Away from the cloistering effects of wedding guests and the party.

She's been home for five days and already felt as though it was time to leave.

*But I won't.*

She had a month. Four weeks to recharge and pull herself together. Not that *she* really believed she needed it. But her boss did. Her therapist did. She had her instructions— go home…go home and spend time with her family. Go home and forget the car crash that had killed a colleague and changed her life.

*So, I'm here.*

She took another sip, finishing her drink. One glass down. Maybe getting drunk would give her some relief from the heavy band of pressure pressing at her temples.

Relief now, perhaps. But regret in morning.

Grace Preston didn't do hangovers. She did fourteen-hour days and skipped lunches and four-inch heels. Vacations were usually a long weekend in her apartment with a laptop and one eye on the stock market.

And Crystal Point, the small beachside Australian town where she'd been born and raised, was a long way from her office, her apartment, her Jimmy Choos and her life in New York.

She took a few steps and cautiously dipped her toes into the ocean. The sound of music and laughter and clinking crockery faded as she headed farther from the huge tent and the celebration of Evie and Scott's wedding. The stars above seemed particularly bright, like they were mocking her, like they knew all her secrets.

Like they knew she wasn't quite whole and there was a tiny window of emptiness aimed directly in the center of her chest. Maybe it was the happiness radiating from her sister that had Grace thinking things she wouldn't normally think.

With a new husband and a baby on the way, Evie had never looked happier.

While Grace had never been more alone in her life.

The fact her boss knew as much was the reason she was back. She was home to recharge and be with the people who loved her. Not that she was about to admit that to anyone anytime soon. Her family thought she was simply home for the wedding and an extended vacation.

She kicked at the tide with her toes and gasped as cold water splashed up her calf, but then ventured in a little more. When she took a swallow of champagne the bubbles zinged up her nose and down her throat. A couple more glasses, she thought, and she might be on her way to sweet oblivion.

The idea made her laugh and she heard the sound echo and then ripple and somehow quietly disappear into the night as she took another step into the water.

Across from the river mouth, where the waterway met the sea, was Jay's Island. It had been part of the mainland once, but years of sand trenching to allow sugar cane ferries to pass had created a gulf between the two banks. Now it was home to nesting herons and sea turtles. When she was young she'd swum the distance, not put off by the fast current that dragged many swimmers along. But she hadn't done that in a long time.

Despite what some people believed, Grace didn't hate Crystal Point. She just had little in common with the small beachside community that boasted a population of barely eight hundred residents. Not after so many years anyway. Time had a way of creating distance and building walls. Grace simply didn't fit in. She never had.

"Don't think I'm gonna jump in and save you if you fall in and get pulled down by the riptide, *Princess*," she heard a deep and infuriatingly familiar voice say from behind her.

"I have no intention of ruining a perfectly good suit because you can't hold your liquor."

Grace swiveled in shock at the sudden intrusion and almost toppled over. Clenching her toes into the sand for balance, she moved up the bank to where Cameron Jakowski stood about ten feet away.

She scowled and fought a guilty look at the glass and bottle clutched between her fingers. She absolutely would not rise to his *Princess* jibe.

"What do you want, *Hot Tub?*"

She saw his smile in the moonlight, knew instinctively that his velvet brown eyes would light up, ready for battle with her. They had always called one another names—always worked out new ways to needle each other. *Hot Tub, Princess*—silly names meant to antagonize.

"Just making sure you don't drown."

Grace shrugged her bare shoulders. "I didn't realize you cared."

He came closer. "It's a wedding. I doubt Evie and Scott would want their celebration ruined by your carelessness."

Grace's temper simmered. "I'm not acting the least bit careless," she said through clenched teeth. "And I'm perfectly sober."

He looked at the bottle. "Prove it," he challenged. "Walk a straight line."

Grace bit back a scowl. "I'll do no such thing. You're not on duty now."

He chuckled and Grace forced herself to *not* think about how sexy it sounded. Okay—so he had a great smile and a handsome face and filled out his police officer's uniform as faultlessly as he did the suit he wore. She'd have to be comatose not to notice.

"So, why are you hiding out here anyway?"

Grace moved up the sand. "Who says I'm hiding?"

Cameron hooked a thumb over one shoulder. "The party's that way."

She shrugged. "Maybe I'm not in the mood for a party."

"Nothing's that simple with you."

Grace bristled. "Leave me alone. I don't want to argue with you."

Cameron stepped closer. "Now I know there's definitely something wrong with you. What's eating you tonight?"

"Nothing," she lied. "I'm my usual happy self."

"And now you're lying your shoes off."

Grace tugged at the hem off her dress and exposed her feet. "I'm not wearing shoes," she announced, holding herself upright despite a sudden surge of wooziness.

Of course, he knew that. He was a groomsman and she'd been partnered with him most of the afternoon. He'd already smirked when he'd spotted her bare feet and purple-painted toenails as she'd taken his arm to walk toward the altar.

*Because Grace Preston didn't bare anything in public.*

And Cameron knew that.

She glared at him some more. "I don't know why the men got to keep their shoes on. Anyway, I'll probably step on a stonefish and that will be the end of me."

Cameron laughed. "So much drama over a pair of missing shoes. Come on, I'll walk you back."

Grace shook her head. "No, thanks—I'll stay here. I've had about all the marital bliss I can stand for one evening."

He was close now and Grace could see the curious expression on his face. "Are you jealous Evie's married?"

Was she? It seemed like everyone was getting married lately and getting their happily-ever-after. First her brother, Noah, had married Callie Jones and now, less than eight months later, Evie was tying the knot with Scott, Callie's younger brother. But no, she wasn't the marrying type.

"Certainly not," she replied quickly and took another sip of

her champagne. "I'm very happy for my sister. I just meant..."
She stopped. There was no way she would explain anything
to Cameron Jakowski. "Nothing. Leave me alone."

He moved toward her again, only this time she didn't step
back. Toe-to-toe, he stood close to eight inches taller than her
and without shoes it was impossible for Grace to stare him
down without tilting her head up.

"And what if you go back into the water and get swept
away by the current?" he inquired. "I don't want that on my
conscience. I'm staying."

Grace shrugged. "Suit yourself," she said as she moved
up the bank some more and headed toward a small cluster of
rocks. She sat on the largest one and refilled her glass. "Want
a shot?" she asked, holding out the bottle.

Cameron followed her steps and took the bottle. "I reckon
you've had about enough of that." He dropped it onto the sand.

Grace watched the champagne seep away. "You're ruining my evening."

"Your evening looked well and truly ruined before you
wandered off down here."

She frowned. "Are you spying on me?"

Cameron laughed. "Hardly—but you did bail on our dance."

"I didn't want to dance," she told him flatly. "With you or
anyone else," she added.

Being partnered with Cameron for the entire celebration
had been more than she could stand. Not only because she
wasn't in any mood to combat his sarcasm or insults, but because the happy smiles and animated chatter of the wedding
party had felt like a cloistering blanket around her shoulders. Since the accident she'd become less adept at handling
crowds. Less inclined to make pointless conversation.

"You know, it wouldn't hurt you to open up a bit."

Grace almost choked on her champagne. Was he reading
her mind? "To you? You're joking, right?"

He shrugged. "Why not?"

"Because you're *you*." She shook her head. "And you and I are like...oil and water."

He stepped closer and thrust his hands in his pockets. "It's a double-edged sword," he said quietly.

Grace stared into her glass. "I have no idea what that's supposed to mean."

"Sure you do," he flipped back. "Admit it, *Princess*—fighting with me gets you all worked up."

Grace wasn't admitting anything. "You're imagining things. Not everything's about you. And stop calling me *Princess*."

"Stop calling me *Hot Tub*."

*Gridlock.*

As usual.

He didn't move. He stood in front of her, smiling, making Grace so mad she was tempted to toss her remaining drink in his direction. For sixteen years they'd been stuck in this groove—hurling insults, sticking it to one another at every opportunity.

But a lifetime ago it had been different. He was her brother's best friend and because of that relationship she'd known him since she was five years old. She'd liked him back then. He hadn't teased her for her bookish ways as her brother did. By the time she was preparing to leave for boarding school liking him had turned into a crush. But she didn't dare admit it or imagine he felt the same way. She left for school and took her silly dreams with her. Nothing had prepared her for the night of her sixteenth birthday when he'd unexpectedly kissed her for the first time. When school was over she'd returned to Crystal Point to take a break before she headed off to college and in those few months they'd dated one another. Cameron Jakowski had been her first real boyfriend. Her first kiss. The one man she'd never quite been able to forget.

"What's really going on with you, Grace?"

Her back straightened, shoving her into the present. "Spare me your fake concern."

He stepped closer. "It's not fake."

Grace didn't believe him. "Like you care?"

He laughed. "C'mon, Grace—lighten up. You're not in your swanky office now. There's no one to impress by pretending you've got it all together."

Grace stilled. His words hit a raw nerve. Because she'd heard the same ones from the therapist her boss had *insisted* she visit. But Cameron didn't know that. No one knew. The terrible accident and the month afterward where she'd returned to work and pretended none of it had happened, or the way she'd spectacularly unraveled in front of a client. She needed to lie through her teeth—for her own sake. "I always have it together—you know that."

"Do I? I know that you've been hanging around down here for the past hour. I know that you've barely cracked a smile all afternoon, at your own sister's wedding. I know that you're unhappy even if you don't have the courage to admit it."

Grace glared at him, hating she felt so transparent in front of Cameron, hating he could see through her. "And I know that if I admit to anything you'll just use it against me. No, thanks." She got to her feet and stumbled.

He grasped her arm quickly. "Steady," he said as he held her.

Grace tried to pull away but he held her firm. Something uncurled low in her belly, warming her blood. A familiar sensation she experienced whenever he was close. It unnerved her and she fought the feeling. "Let me go."

"You'll fall over."

"So, I'll fall." She was suddenly powerless as one strong arm came around her waist.

"I'd catch you," he said quietly.

Grace frowned. "Let me go...please."

But she wasn't afraid. She'd never feared Cameron. Despite their differences, she'd always trusted him. Grace felt the nearness of him and fought the sudden warmth spreading across her skin. That he could do this to her—make her boil with fury one moment and burn with awareness the next—only added to her resentment and determination to keep as far away from him as possible. He was the only man she'd ever known who'd been able to do that to her. The only man she'd ever thought could see through her, know her and work her out.

"Don't..."

"I'm not doing anything."

"You are. You do. You always do. I just want..." She stopped, stalled and felt herself get dragged into meeting his eyes. She was flustered, uneasy. "I can't..."

"What is it?" he asked softly. "What's going on in that beautiful head of yours?"

Grace's resistance crumbled. The champagne she'd had suddenly freed up her tongue. "I just... I don't belong here," she admitted and pulled herself from his grasp as she stepped backward. "I don't belong anywhere."

Cameron's hands burned from the feel of Grace's skin and he clenched his fists at his sides. The pain in her voice knocked through him, settling behind his ribs in a way that made him think about every feeling he'd had for her—and buried.

"What do you mean?"

She turned away, clutching her arms around herself. "Nothing," she said quietly.

Cameron pushed the heels of his shoes up from sinking in the sand and pressed on. "What do you mean you don't belong?"

Grace twirled around and her long dress billowed around her knees. "Why do you care?"

Why indeed? He shouldn't. Grace was nothing but trouble. A workaholic ice princess who had little time for anyone. *Me included.* He'd found that out the hard way. Beautiful beyond words, smart and independent—and about as warm as an Arctic winter. The perfect antidote for all his fantasies. Wanting her was about as sensible as wanting acid rain.

He shrugged. "Friendly concern."

Her beautiful face looked almost luminescent in the moonlight as she shot him a death stare. "Don't be nice to me," she said quietly, looking suspicious. "We're not friends and I just—"

"We were more than friends," he said and took hold of her hand despite his best intentions to not touch her. "Once."

She stared at their linked hands and this time, she didn't pull away. Cameron's fingertips tingled. He knew that would happen if he touched Grace…expected it…didn't like it one bit but chalked it up to chemistry and tried not to let it mess with his mind. Over the years there had been the odd touch between them, the chance gesture of hands brushing…and every time it was the same. The same vibration rattled inside him, over his skin, through his blood. He knew it wasn't like that for her, of course. Grace was supercool and controlled, with perfectly straight dark hair, immaculate clothes and haunting green eyes—like a mannequin on display. A mere touch wouldn't jangle Grace. But he remembered what it was like to touch her, to kiss her, to hold her in his arms. Those memories were burned into his soul.

As expected, she pulled away. "A lifetime ago."

Her dismissal cut deep. She'd left him without looking

back all those years ago and as much as he wanted to deny it, that rejection still stung. He smiled because he knew it would infuriate her. "So, explain what you meant about not belonging anywhere?"

"No. It was nothing." She shrugged lightly. "And now, if you don't mind, I need to get back to the party."

He didn't believe her for a second. So he pushed. Because he could. Because he wanted to know what was going on inside her beautiful head. "So, has this got anything to do with that suit you've shacked up with?"

Her lips came together. "Erik," she said after a moment. "We broke up a year ago. And we were never *shacked up*. We both kept our own apartments."

She crossed her arms. The movement pushed her breasts upward and Cameron did his best to ignore the swell of cleavage rising up and down with each breath she took. He'd never met the other man, since Grace had kept him under wraps in New York. But Cameron had heard about him from her brother. He was stupidly pleased the suit wasn't in the picture anymore. "You didn't answer the question."

"Because it's a moot point." Grace scowled, but somehow managed to still look beautiful. "And I really don't want to talk to you about my...love life."

Cameron bristled. Did he even think Grace capable of love? "So you loved him?"

"No," she replied swiftly. "I meant...I meant I have no intention of talking to you about him. Now, would you ignore everything I've said and leave me alone?"

Cameron wanted to laugh. "Ignore you? Yeah, right."

Her gaze sharpened. "Ignoring me isn't usually a problem for you. Except of course when you're making fun or insulting me."

"It goes both ways, Grace."

She moved her feet and seemed to come a little closer.

"I guess it does." She dropped her arms. "It only happens with you."

"Do you ever wonder why?"

She raised one perfectly arched brow. "Why would I bother?"

"It might explain one of the great mysteries of the world."

She laughed humorlessly. He could sense her thinking of some kind of cutting retort and wasn't disappointed. "I don't want to rain on your monumental ego, but I really don't have the time to waste wondering about things like that."

"So you never think about it?"

She stilled. "About what?"

"You and me?"

"We were over a long time ago. It was a silly teenage summer romance. I hardly remember."

Her response pushed his buttons. Because he didn't quite believe her. The tension between them had never waned. Every time she returned to Crystal Point, every time they spoke, every time he caught her stare from across a room, the awareness between them was still there. He straightened his shoulders. Down deep, in that place he'd shut off because it stirred up a whole lot of hurt, Cameron remembered what it felt like to want her so much it haunted his dreams. "Maybe you need a reminder."

She faced him with an indignant glare. "And what exactly do you propose?"

"Propose?" He smiled. "Is that what you're after, *Princess*—a proposal? Couldn't you get the suit to the altar?"

Her green eyes flashed. "I have no desire or plans in that regard. I'd think you'd know that better than anyone."

He did. He wasn't likely to forget. They'd started dating when she'd finished high school. She'd come home from boarding school that final time and he'd waited two weeks before asking her out. Three months into their relationship she'd bailed. She wanted a career and a different life…a life that didn't include a small-town police officer. A life that didn't include him or marriage or the possibility of children in the future. She'd made her intentions abundantly clear. Grace Preston wanted a career. And that's *all* she wanted. She'd left Crystal Point for New York without looking back.

Except for now. This Grace was someone new. Someone who didn't seem like she had her usual ice running through her veins. Grace never did vulnerable. And Cameron wanted to know more.

"The corporate life is still giving you everything you need, is it?" he asked, referring to her highly successful job as a finance broker.

"Of course."

"So your little outburst earlier, what was that about?"

Her brows came up. "Are we back on that subject again? It was nothing. Forget it."

"And let you off the hook?" He rocked on his heels. "No chance."

"Haven't you got anything better to do with that mouth of yours than run off with it at me about my life?"

He did. Absolutely. And her words were like a red cape to a bull.

"Did you have something in mind?"

"No, I don't," she said with a caustic smile. "And don't get any ideas."

He laughed at her prickles. Only Grace could make him do that. *Only ever Grace.* "I could kiss you," he teased. "That would shut me up."

She stepped back. "Don't even think about it."

It really was all the challenge he needed and Cameron moved closer. "Grace, you know me better than that."

Her green eyes were alight with fire and defiance. "You're right, I do know you. I know you've got a reputation for nailing anything in a skirt. The last thing I want to be is a notch on your bedpost, Jakowski…so back off."

"You shouldn't believe everything you hear." Cameron placed his hands on her shoulders. She didn't resist. Didn't move. "Kiss me, Grace?"

She shook her head slightly. "No."

The air shifted, creating a swift, uncommonly hot vacuum which somehow seemed to draw them closer. Their bodies brushed and it spiked his blood. He shouldn't want this… shouldn't do this. But everything about Grace Preston took him to another level of awareness. It was almost primitive in its intensity and it made him forget all his good intentions to stay as far away from her as possible.

"Then I'll kiss you."

"I won't kiss you back," she whispered, but he felt her slide a little closer.

Cameron's libido did a wild leap as he moved his arms around her, bringing them together. "Sure you will."

"I won't," she said boldly. "I hate you, remember?"

"You'll get over it," he said smoothly and moved one hand to her nape. For twenty years he'd wanted her like no other woman. For sixteen years he'd been angry at her for breaking his heart.

Grace stared up at him, her green eyes shining and wide in her face.

She looked more beautiful than he'd ever seen her. More desirable. More everything. Without thinking…with nothing but feeling and the need to suddenly possess her, Cameron claimed her lips with his own.

## *Chapter Two*

*I will not make out with Cameron Jakowski.*

Too late. Grace allowed his mouth to slant over hers and her breath left her sharply.

*Maybe just for a moment...*

Because he still knew how to kiss. And she hadn't been kissed by Cameron in such a long time....

Her resistance faded and she opened her mouth, inviting him inside. Blood rushed low down in her belly, spiking her temperature upward like a roller coaster moving way too fast. Grace floated along and was quickly caught up in the deep-rooted pleasure which unexpectedly tingled across her skin. The kiss deepened and Grace felt his tongue roll gently around hers. It was so incredibly arousing she couldn't prevent a low moan from escaping deep in her throat.

*I should stop this...right now.* But she didn't. She just let herself float on a sigh and kissed him back. Her arms moved upward and she curled her fingers into his shoulders. The movement brought their bodies together and Grace melted against him. *Strong and safe.* The words spun around in her head and rocked her to the core. Because she knew she'd only ever felt that way with Cameron. Not with Erik. Not with any man she'd ever been with.

His arms came around her and one hand settled on her hip. And still he kissed her. Grace clung to him as heat charged between them. His touch became firmer and he bunched a handful of her dress in his fist. The tempo between them altered slightly, and the hot surge of desire fanned to life.

He said something against her mouth—her name— something…she wasn't sure. But it fueled the growing need she had to feel his touch. She lifted her leg and wrapped it against him. Her dress rose up and she shuddered when his hand made contact with the soft skin behind her knee. It felt so good to be with him like this, even though some faraway voice told her it was madness. Every part of her came alive when he touched her and she arched her back with a hazy, wanting compliance.

"Grace," he said, leaving her mouth for a moment. He trailed a line of kisses across her cheek and toward the sensitive spot below her ear. "I think it would be a good idea if we stopped…."

Grace turned her head so their lips met again. She didn't want to stop. She only wanted to feel. "No," she whispered into his mouth. "Don't stop."

"You'll hate me tomorrow," he said softly against her craving lips.

"I hate you now…"

She felt his smile against her mouth.

*He's right, we have to stop…*

Only Cameron's touch was mesmerizing and his kiss had her longing for more. His fingertips burned across her skin in an erotic trail, moving higher, and the blood in her veins boiled over in a powerful surge of narcotic pleasure. She felt his hand on the top of her thigh and she pushed closer. He was obviously as hotly aroused as she was and the notion drove Grace beyond rational thought, beyond reason. His palm curved around her bottom and he drew her hard against his body. Need uncurled low down, liquefying her bones. She groaned as his mouth sought hers again and kissed him back with a hunger that startled her, entwining her tongue with his. She was dazed, on fire, out of control. Grace's knees almost gave way when his fingers traced the edge of her lace panties. *I shouldn't want this. I shouldn't feel this turned on.* But she was so aroused, so completely oblivious to anything other the sudden and unexpected need to be taken to places she suspected he'd effortlessly be able to take her.

But reality intruded and brought her back to earth with a resounding, wrenching thud.

The music resonating from the wedding reception area came to an abrupt halt and the silence was suddenly deafening. "Oh, my God," Grace moaned as she jerked her mouth from his. "My speech!"

Cameron released her. "What?"

Grace staggered back and shoved her dress down her thighs with shaking hands. "I have to give a speech. I'm the maid of honor. I have to get back."

He looked annoyingly calm. "Okay, we'll go back."

"No," Grace said on a rush of breath. "I'm not walking back up there with you. I look like…" She pushed a hand into her hair and was relieved to discover that the up style was still in its right position. But her blood raced, her breath was shallow and she was certain her mouth looked as though it had been well and truly plundered. "I must look like I've been—"

"You have been," he agreed quietly, seeming completely cool and relaxed. "Don't stress, *Princess*. You look fine—as picture-perfect as always."

Grace crossed her arms and glanced toward the reception area. The big white tent stood out like a beacon in the moonlight. She heard someone speaking into a microphone and quickly recognized her father's steady voice. "I need to get back. And don't follow me."

He didn't respond immediately. He just looked at her. Looked *through* her was more the point. Humiliation burned across her skin like an out-of-control brush fire.

*This was not supposed to happen. I didn't come home for this. Nothing will stop me from getting my life and career back on track.*

He grabbed the bottle and glass from the sand. "Let's go," he said quietly.

Grace considered some kind of cold retort, but failed to find one.

*Cameron Jakowski had his hand up my dress.*

"All right," she said with a deliberate tilt of her chin and tried not to think about how good his hand had felt. "We won't ever mention this again."

"Sure we will."

Grace lifted her hem fractionally and took a few steps up the sand. "We won't," she said defiantly. "*I* won't. I intend to forget this ever happened."

"Good luck with that."

Grace stomped along the sand, headed for the boat ramp and walked back toward the reception. As she'd suspected, her father's proud speech was in full swing and Grace circumnavigated the huge tent and slipped through an opening behind the wedding table as discreetly as she could.

But Evie's hawkeyed radar caught a glimpse of her immediately and Grace did her best to squash a fresh wave of embarrassment from heating her cheeks. Evie raised both her brows inquiringly and Grace managed a barely decipherable

shake of her head. It didn't help that Cameron chose that moment to make his entrance through the same opening.

*Busted...*

The look on her sister's face was unmistakable. She knew
Evie would demand answers at some point. That was Evie's
way. Grace steeled herself with a deep breath and took her
conspicuously empty seat at the table. Cameron did the same
a few seats away and she used every inch of effort to not look
at him. Instead, she concentrated her attention on her father's
heartfelt speech.

When it was her turn to say a few words, Grace stood and
took the microphone from her father and softly kissed his
cheek. All the guests clearly waited for her to speak. And
she meant to. Only she made a fatal mistake and glanced at
Cameron. And damn him—he smiled, winked and made her
forget every word she'd planned to say in honor of the bride
and groom.

Nothing came out, only a squeak, a kind of strangled sound
that a distressed cat might make.

And it was pain-in-her-neck, thorn-in-her-side Cameron
Jakowski's fault.

Supercool Grace Preston was at a loss for words. Any
other time Cameron might have been happy about that. But
tonight...not so much. He could still taste her lovely mouth;
still feel the silky texture of her skin against his hands.

One minute they were talking, the next they were kissing
like a couple of horny teenagers. Cameron couldn't remember
the last time he'd felt like that. The last time he'd *done* that.

And he certainly hadn't expected to do it with Miss Icy
Britches.

He'd mostly kept his hands to himself when they were dating. They'd made out plenty of times—but never quite like
what had happened on the beach. She'd wanted to wait to

make love and he'd respected her wishes, although he'd imagined a future together—a wedding, a wedding *night*. Until Grace had informed him of her big plans for a career and a future that didn't include Crystal Point or the small-town police officer who wanted to marry her one day.

But right now, she didn't look like the Grace he'd come to resent. It was easier that way, easier not thinking about her perfectly beautiful face and body. And yet his skin felt tight watching her, waiting for her to speak. She was off balance, askew, and he knew it wasn't the champagne doing damage.

It churned something inside him, thinking he was responsible for the kind of hazy, almost lost look on her face as she stared into the microphone. He smiled again, different this time, without mockery, with only the intent to calm her obviously fractured nerves. She met his gaze and they remained like that for a moment, linked by some invisible thread that had nothing to do with the searing kisses they'd shared, or the years of thinly veiled antagonism that had come to define their relationship. He saw her relax, watched as her jaw loosened and then she began to speak.

"Tonight is a celebration," she said and then swallowed hard, as though the words were difficult to say. "Of love. Of trust. Of the commitment between two people."

She went on to talk about the bride and groom, speaking clearly and concisely as she wished the newlyweds a long and happy life. Cameron wondered if she meant it. He'd never heard her speak about love before. When she was done she returned to her seat and didn't spare him another look.

Dessert was served after that and Cameron pushed the sugary sweet around on his plate. The dancing started again and the woman beside him dug him in the ribs with her elbow, but he was in no mood for that either. He declined her invitation and managed a smile when she scooted off her chair.

Mary-Jayne Preston was a pretty brunette with amazing green eyes—and she was Grace's younger sister.

*Grace...*

She didn't like him. He didn't like her. But he'd wanted her and loved her most of his adult life. He thought he was over it. Thought he had it under control.

*Jackass...*

"Why do you look like you want to be somewhere else?"

Cameron turned his head. Noah Preston. His best friend. And Grace's older brother. "You know me and weddings," he replied casually.

The other man ducked into the empty chair beside him. "Are you tempted to take the walk yourself?" Noah asked.

He shrugged to disguise the truth. Because he did want to get married. He wanted a wife and kids and the whole deal. Cameron longed for a family of his own. He was thirty-six years old and had dated a succession of women, none he saw for more than a few months. And none who invaded his deepest dreams like Grace Preston.

He'd built a house designed for a family and lived in it alone. Dated women he knew weren't going to figure permanently in his life. For a long time he'd avoided thinking about marriage and family. Once Grace left Crystal Point he'd pushed his focus into his career as a police officer and tried to forget about her. And their ongoing resentment for one another had fueled that focus. But now he wanted more. More than an empty house when he came home after a long shift at work, more than an empty bed. Or one filled occasionally with someone he barely knew.

He wanted what his parents had. He wanted what his best friend had.

"It's not as bad as you think," Noah said easily. "Actually, it's the smartest move I ever made. You just need to find the right woman."

Noah had married Callie Jones eight months earlier and the stunning, blue-eyed, California horse-riding instructor had transformed his friend's life. His four children had a new mother and Noah had the love of a woman he adored. And with Callie's brother, Scott, now married to Evie, it seemed like everyone around him was getting their happily-ever-after.

*Just not me.*

It made him think of green eyes. *Grace's eyes.* Noah would have a fit if he knew what he was thinking. Or what he'd been doing with her down by the beach.

"I never said it was bad."

Noah laughed. "I'm sure there's some sweet, easygoing girl out there who—"

"I don't want easygoing," he said swiftly. "Or sweet."

*Grace again.* Because Grace wasn't either of those things. She was smart and independent and reserved and coolly argumentative and…

*And she's the only woman I've ever wanted.*

Noah laughed again. "Can't say I blame you. I love my wife's spirit." There was a gleam in his friend's eyes. "Makes life more interesting."

"I'll bet," Cameron said agreeably.

"Were you with Grace earlier?"

Cameron shot a glance at his friend. "For a minute," he said and pushed aside the nagging guilt hitting him between the shoulder blades.

"Something's going on with her," Noah said. "She said she's taking some time off work. But she's not talking about why, not even to Evie or our mother. Maybe breaking up with that attorney has something to do with it."

Cameron remembered what she'd said about the suit and sensed she wasn't all that broken up about it. But what she'd said about not belonging—now that, he was sure, had something to do with her return home. Because it was completely *unlike* Grace to say a thing like that. Noah was right—something *was* going on with her. The Grace he knew didn't show vulnerability. She was ice-cool and resilient. At eighteen she'd walked away from him and Crystal Point and moved to New York and had been there ever since, returning once or twice a year at the most. That was the Grace Preston he understood. Not the vulnerable one moment, hotter than Hades the next kind of woman who'd kissed him back like there was no tomorrow.

Wanting her had made every other woman he'd known pale by comparison. And now he knew one thing—he either had to get Grace out of his head for good…or *get* Grace in his bed and in his life.

She was home, on his turf. Maybe he had a shot. The way she'd kissed him gave him some optimism. That kind of response wasn't fake. And he knew Grace. She wouldn't pretend. Whatever was going on with her, Cameron was determined to find out. She'd resist and fight. She'd make things impossible. She'd cut him down with icy barbs and indifference.

Suddenly that seemed like one hell of an interesting challenge.

Cameron's gaze centered on Grace. She was with Evie, talking close. His shirt collar got uncomfortably tight and irritation uncurled in his chest. Because he would bet right down to his boots that they were talking about him.

"So, what happened?"

Grace tried to escape her sister's viselike grip on her wrist but failed. Evie was persistent when she wanted something. She loved her sister and Evie was the one person she could really talk to. But not about this. Not about Cameron.

"Nothing. We were just talking."

Evie's dramatic brows rose. "Well, I imagine you were doing something with your tongues."

Grace flushed and tacked herself at Evie's side to hide from Cameron's view in case he looked her way. Her sister's seven months pregnant belly was a good shield. "I don't want to talk about it."

Evie chuckled. "Oh, no—you don't get out of it that easy. I want details."

"I won't say what…" Grace's response faded on her lips. "Okay," she admitted. "So we might have…"

"Might have?" Evie interrupted without batting a lash.

"We kissed," she whispered into her sister's ear, feeling about sixteen years old. She certainly wasn't about to admit to anything else. "And that's all I'm saying."

Evie hauled Grace into the corner so they had more privacy. "You kissed Cameron?" she squealed. "Oh, my God! I can't believe it."

*Neither can I.*

"Well, I mean I *can* believe it," Evie said in a wicked whisper. "Did it bring back a whole lot of memories?"

Of course it did. But she wasn't about to say that. Grace regretted ever telling her sister about the three-month relationship she'd had with Cameron—about the kisses and gentle touches and soft moans as they made out in the front seat of his car. Because it brought back other memories as well—the way she'd left, the way she'd run when she'd sensed he was getting serious. It was so long ago. In a different life. Wanting Cameron now was sheer madness. It was champagne that had made her behave so impulsively. And she hadn't been with a man since forever. No wonder she'd acted like she did. She only hoped no one else saw their conspicuous entrance. The last thing she wanted was the Crystal Point rumor mill churning out theories about what had happened between her and the charming and popular Sergeant Jakowski down by the beach.

Everyone liked Cameron. She knew some of what he did in the community—the volunteer work at the surf club, the time he spent with kids from the Big Brothers Big Sisters program. An all-around good guy. Honest, honorable and socially conscious. Grace knew it about him and had always felt like he was rubbing her nose in the fact. Irrational as it was, he made her feel selfish and, worse…self-absorbed. Like her life was meaningless and superficial. He never said it of course, rarely spoke to her unless to demean her fondness for pricey footwear or call her *Princess* in that infuriating way.

"Can I steal my beautiful bride away for a dance?" Scott Jones approached and took Evie's hand.

"Of course," Grace said and smiled when she saw the glow on her sister's face. Evie had found true love with the handsome, California firefighter. "We were done anyway."

Evie smiled. "We'll talk later," she said and allowed herself to be swept away.

Grace remained where she was and studied the crowd for a moment. The usual suspects were in attendance and a few she'd never met before, mostly friends and colleagues of the groom who'd traveled from Los Angeles. She spotted her younger sister Mary-Jayne, or M.J. as she was affectionately called, dancing closely with Gabe Vitali, the best man and cousin of the groom. She was supposed to have been partnered with the outrageously good-looking American, but M.J. had pleaded they swap groomsmen and Grace agreed, unable to refuse her sister's request.

"They make a cute couple."

Grace froze. Cameron had approached and edged alongside her. She glanced at him and he nodded toward M.J. and Gabe. "I'm no judge."

"And yet you're usually so good at it."

It was a dig, but he was smiling so she let it pass. She wasn't about to have an argument with him in front of so many people. "Did you want something?"

"Just to see how you were doing."

Grace raised both shoulders. "As you can see, I'm perfectly fine."

"Good speech by the way."

"Thank you." She took a deep breath. No thanks to him. "I should get back to—"

He laid one finger against her wrist. "I think we should talk, Grace."

Awareness crept along her skin and she tingled where they touched. "I'd rather not."

"So, where are you staying?"

Grace swiveled on her heels to face him. "At Evie's."

"While she and Scott are on their honeymoon?" His brows came up. "Are they leaving you in charge of the B and B?"

The query in his voice was skeptical. "Don't sound so surprised. I'm not totally inept, you know."

He smiled to expose perfectly straight teeth. "I think it's good of you to help out."

She pulled away from his touch, but Grace couldn't ignore the way he watched her and her body was quickly on high alert.

"So, shall we resume our earlier conversation?" he asked.

Grace stepped back. "Don't push it."

"You know, you look really beautiful when your cage is rattled."

"You're an ass, Jakowski."

"And you're hiding something," he replied. "Whatever it is, Grace, you may as well come clean."

Heat crept up her neck and she hated that he could do that. "*If* there was anything wrong, I certainly wouldn't be sharing it with you."

"Your family is concerned about you. Noah thinks you're nursing a broken heart after breaking up with the suit."

"I'm not."

"I know."

He said the words with such arrogant authority that Grace glared at him. "I wish you wouldn't do that."

"Do what?"

"Act as though you know or care. I'll talk to my brother."

"When?"

Grace's skin burned. "When I'm ready."

"You've been home almost a week, seems to me like you would have had plenty of opportunity to tell your family what's going on."

"Stay out of it," she warned.

"Or what?" He chuckled. He was toying with her. As usual. "Ah, *Princess,* you're about as wound up as a spinning top at the moment."

"No thanks to you," she fired back and crossed her arms.

He smiled again. "By the way, you owe me a dance."

Dancing? After what had happened on the beach she had no intention of falling into his arms again. "You don't have a chance of getting me on the dance floor."

"Things have a way of changing," he said and gently took hold of her elbow. "As we discovered earlier."

The kiss. The touching. The insane desire that had taken hold. Of course he'd remind her about it. "Don't imagine for one minute that we'll be repeating that craziness anytime soon."

"Are you sure about that, Grace?"

She stuck out her chin. "Positive."

"Such confidence," he said in that vague, annoying way of his. "So, about that dance?"

She clung to her resolve. "No."

"I could beg and embarrass you."

Grace refused to react. "You mean embarrass yourself. And surely there are other women here you can try to charm the pants off other than me."

He laughed and she hated that a few people looked in their direction. "Is that what you think I'm doing, Grace? Trying to get your pants off?"

She cast him a sharp look. "Try your best, *Hot Tub*."

He grinned at her attempt to antagonize. But she knew he would win out. She'd called him the ridiculous name for a decade because he'd installed a huge spa bath at the house he'd built and her brother teased that it was to impress women. She hadn't liked the idea then. And she liked it even less now.

"Are you throwing down the gauntlet, Grace?"

"Not at all." She managed to pull away and put some space between them. "I'm...tired," she said and shook her head. "Too tired to play games."

"Then tell me what's going on with you. If you do I might be inclined to leave you alone."

Exasperated by his persistent badgering, Grace threw up her hands. "So, what do you want to know?"

His gaze narrowed. "Why you've come back for so long this time?"

"Because this is my home."

He clearly didn't believe that for a second. "Last I heard New York was your home, Grace. Crystal Point was the place you couldn't get away from fast enough."

It was a direct hit. She knew what he meant. Her career was the reason she'd left Crystal Point—the reason she'd put an end to their relationship all those years ago. She'd been overwhelmed, crowded, hemmed in...everything she didn't want to be. Leaving had been her salvation. And her career had panned out exactly as she'd dreamed it would. Until the car wreck that had changed her life.

Grace's back stiffened. "You know why I left. I wanted…
I wanted…"

"Bright lights, big city."

She stilled. Quiet stretched between them, like brittle
elastic. The music seemed to fade and Grace experienced a
strange tightening behind her ribs. "It was never that simple."

"Yes, it was, Grace." His voice was velvet-smooth, his expression unreadable. "You knew what you wanted. What you
didn't. And who you didn't."

She looked into his eyes. It sounded so black-and-white.
But nothing was simple anymore. And she didn't have the
courage to admit the truth—that she'd gone to New York
to make her parents proud and become everything they'd
hoped she would become…or that now she'd come home to
save her life.

## Chapter Three

On Sunday morning at her sister's bed-and-breakfast, Grace reorganized the upstairs linen cupboard, alphabetized Evie's cookbooks and by eleven o'clock was sitting on the sofa watching a corny movie on a cable channel.

Anything to take her mind off the job she'd left in New York, the empty apartment that had never really felt like a home and the accident that killed her work colleague. An accident that had altered her in so many ways. Before that awful day she'd been in control of her life and future. There were no question marks. No uncertainty. At least none she was prepared to admit. She had known her trajectory. Her plan.

*You knew what you wanted. And who you didn't.*

Cameron's words rolled around in her head.

Because there had been the sting of truth in those words.

When they'd dated, when he'd said he had serious feelings for her and wanted to talk about their future together, she'd panicked and cut him down immediately. And as she sat in the lotus position on the sofa and stared absently at the television, Grace remembered what she'd said to him in stunning Technicolor.

*"I'm just not interested in anything serious. Especially not with a small-town cop. I'm getting out of Crystal Point as soon as I can. There's nothing and no one that could ever hold me here."*

Insensitive and cruel. And a pivotal moment in her life. What if she'd said something else to him? What if she'd had the courage to acknowledge her deepest, secret feelings and fears? And if she hadn't left Crystal Point when she did, would she have felt even more trapped in their relationship, perhaps their marriage, had it ever come to that?

Grace sat back on the sofa and uncurled her legs.

Marriage had never figured in her life. Erik, who was as focused on his career as she was, had never mentioned it. Before Erik, she'd had a three-year relationship with Dennis Collier. The handsome and successful orthopedic surgeon had asked her twice to marry him—both times she'd insisted she was happy with the tempo of their relationship. She worked long hours and kept her own apartment. Toward the end they'd go for days without seeing one another. Eventually Dennis had traded her for a third-year resident at the hospital where he worked. Within six months of their breakup she heard he'd married and had a baby on the way.

The news hadn't torn her up. She'd genuinely cared for Dennis—but knew it wasn't the kind of feeling that could sustain her for a lifetime. There were feelings, certainly... but love? Grace wasn't sure she even knew how to be in love. Long ago she'd run from those feelings, terrified they'd trap her, make her less than whole and dilute her ambition. She'd wanted a career. That's what she'd planned for. That's what her parents expected of her. Not marriage. Not babies. Not Crystal Point. That legacy was left to her brother and sisters.

Noah took over running the family business and Evie was the original Earth Mother. While M.J. waltzed through life as a free spirit, making jewelry and saving the world with her causes. She was Grace Preston—smart, successful... *untouchable*.

Her cell rang, interrupting her thoughts, and she grabbed it from the coffee table.

"Hey, *Princess*."

She bit back a startled gasp and took a deep breath. Strange that Cameron should telephone when her head was full of thoughts of him. "Would you stop calling me that?"

Cameron laughed softly. "I'll do my best. So, how are things?"

"Since last night?" she shot back and ignored the rapid thump of her heart.

He was silent for a moment and Grace could swear he was smiling. "Come down to the surf club this afternoon."

"What?"

"The surf club," he said again. "I want to show you something."

"What kind of something?"

"Something you'll want to see."

Grace colored hotly. The conversation was oddly flirtatious and she was startled by how it made her feel. "I...I don't think so."

"Oh, come on, Grace," he said and laughed. "Live dangerously. You never know—you might like it."

"No."

"You'll miss seeing something great."

Again, more flirting, more...*something*. He was infuriating.

Grace made an unglamorous grunting sound. "Whatever game you're playing, Jakowski, it's not the least bit funny."

"Game?" he said and chuckled. "That's harsh, *Princess*. You need to learn to trust."

He was laughing at her. As always. Her fingers turned white where she gripped the phone. "Jerk!"

She disconnected and wondered why he was the one person who could push her buttons so easily. And then she wondered why she cared that he did.

Her mother came to visit a little later and Grace made some tea and took a spot opposite at the big scrubbed table in the kitchen. Barbara Preston was the übermother. A career teacher, she'd managed to raise four children and work full-time until her retirement a few years earlier.

"So, what's going on, Grace?"

She knew that tone—knew her mother had something to say. "Nothing," she replied and poured the tea.

Her mother made a disbelieving sound and grabbed a mug. "Grace, I know something's up with you. You've been home a week now. And other than at Christmastime every few years, you never stay this long."

Grace looked at her mother. "I'm fine. Just taking a break."

It wasn't exactly a lie. She *was* on a break. A forced break. After the accident, her employer had insisted she see a therapist. Half a dozen visits later the counselor had recommended time off from her hectic job as a finance broker and her life in New York. Grace had resisted until she'd unexpectedly fallen apart one afternoon while meeting a client. Thankfully, the client hadn't been appalled by her unstoppable tears, and instead had called on her secretary, who'd then informed her boss. Another therapy session followed and without any choice but to agree, the week she'd planned to come home for Evie's wedding turned into a month.

"I'm worried about you."

"There's no need," Grace assured her mother. "I was a little burned-out, that's all."

"You're not sick or anything?"

"No," she said quickly. There was no point mentioning the accident. She knew her mother would only worry. "I'm perfectly healthy."

Barbara looked at her and smiled. "Okay, I'll stop smothering. I did think it might have been a man who brought you back home."

In a way it had been. Richard Bennett had been a colleague in the firm where she worked. He was also a devoted husband and father. A forty-nine-year-old man who hadn't deserved his fate.

"There's no man in my life," she said quietly. "And Erik left a long time ago."

"Are you looking for a relationship?"

It was an unexpected question. Her mother never meddled in her love life. And since her family had known of her career ambitions from a young age, her decision to move to New York was never challenged. "You know how I feel about all that."

Barbara sighed and as always, Grace wished she knew how to really connect with her mother. Evie knew how. And Mary-Jayne. They fit in. Grace had always felt like she was watching her family from the outside. Oh, she was loved, she knew that. But being part of things? That was different. She'd never belonged in Crystal Point. New York had embraced her in ways the tiny town never had. Until she'd been forced to abandon that life.

Now she felt as misplaced as she had all those years ago when she'd been sent to boarding school. As a child she'd shown an aptitude for math and music and at twelve had been enrolled into a school that offered a curriculum designed for gifted children. She'd spent six years at that school, coming back only for the holidays. When her high school years were over, Grace had returned to Crystal Point for a few months. It was during that time that she began dating Cameron. Three months later she'd packed her bags and moved to New York.

Sixteen years on and she still didn't know where she fit in.

"Marriage isn't a prison sentence," her mother said gently.

Grace nodded. "I know. But not everyone gets it all. And I'm not the settle down, picket fence type."

"I only want to see you happy."

"I know that, too," Grace replied. "And I am," she said and smiled. Not exactly the truth, but she wasn't about to burden her mother with her problems. She needed to forget. Not dwell.

"Sometimes I think…" Her mother's voice faded for a moment. "I think that you were too young to have left home when you did all those years ago."

"I was strong-willed," Grace said, and managed a smile. "And I wanted to go."

Her mother patted her hand. "I know you did. And your dad and I were so proud of you for having the courage to follow your dreams. And we're still proud, Grace. You always were our shining star."

She'd heard it before. That's why she'd been sent to boarding school while the other Preston children remained in Crystal Point. *Grace is special. Grace is so smart. Grace will have a stellar career in whatever field she chooses.* How often had she heard those words while she was growing up and attending the school? Within six months she'd been pushed up a grade and then spent the following five years as the youngest student in her class. She knew it had cost her parents tens of thousands every year for her tuition. She owed them a lot for giving her the education she'd had. But there were also times when she'd wished she was simply ordinary Grace Preston.

Without the high IQ. Without the pressure to succeed and make good grades.

She'd never told her parent's how she'd felt. There never seemed the right time. To complain would make her ungrateful, undeserving. And once school was over she just wanted to move on from those unhappy years.

When her mother left, Grace changed into designer jeans, high-end mules and a white, immaculately pressed T-shirt. She found a visor hanging on a peg near the back door and positioned it on her head. She needed to walk. To think.

The beach beckoned.

Winter meant fewer swimmers, even though the day was warm and the water temperature would probably be moderate. Grace locked up the private living area upstairs and checked on the single guest who was lazing in the front sunroom. The lone occupant was a gentleman in his sixties who had come to Dunn Inn alone for the first time in ten years, following the death of his wife. Talking with him for a few minutes stretched Grace's emotions and by the time she'd said goodbye and headed outside, her throat was tight and thick. Her nerves were fraught enough and the sad widower somehow pushed her buttons. She took a deep breath and walked across the road. The grassy shoulder led to a long pathway, which ran parallel with the ocean and wound down toward the beach.

Grace followed the trail at a reasonable pace and it took about ten minutes to reach the sandy knolls leading up to the beach. She stalled at the edge of the rise and took a deep breath. The surf club stood to her left.

*I didn't come here for this. For him. I'm not going anywhere near that building.*

Only…she *was* curious.

Grace took a second, shook her shoulders and walked across the path.

\* \* \*

"There's just no way I can do it!"

Cameron bit back an exasperated sigh as seventeen-year-old Emily Maxwell pulled a pile of books from a battered knapsack. "You knew it was going to be difficult."

"But not impossible," she wailed and dumped the bag at her feet. "I'll never learn this stuff in time."

"You've two weeks before you need to sit that makeup exam, Em," he reminded her.

She rolled her eyes toward the toddler playing on a mat in the corner of the room. "And I've got a two-year-old kid to look after. It ain't gonna happen. It's over."

"How about I ask your grandmother to help with the baby?"

Emily shook her head. "She's got my brothers and sister to take care of. And they're all going out to the farm next week."

Cameron had heard the same story all afternoon. The teenager had been given an opportunity to complete a makeup exam that would go toward her final grade. But she'd talked of giving in to the pressure and Cameron knew he needed to do something to stop her from throwing away her chance at an education. He just didn't know what. Emily was the oldest sister of Dylan. Twelve-year-old Dylan was one of his charges in the Big Brother program sponsored by his station. When Cameron inherited Dylan from the retiring sergeant at the station, he also inherited the teenage mother, her ailing grandmother and two other half siblings. Officially Dylan was his Big Brother charge, but the rest of them were in such dire circumstances, Cameron feared they'd all slip through the cracks and end up separated and in social services. They were a loving family, but down on their luck and needing help.

When Pat Jennings got custody of her grandchildren from her drug-addicted and incarcerated daughter, the town rallied together and raised funds enough for a deposit on a small

farm out west. With the house a few months away from being
ready for the families' final move, Cameron knew this was
Emily's last chance to finish high school. If only she could
get past her resistance to study so she could complete the
makeup examination. Emily was intelligent, but lacked confidence. She'd missed classes and failed to finish set assign-
ments throughout the year as she juggled single parenthood.
It was a heavy load for a girl not yet eighteen.

"You have to find the time to study," he said quietly.

"It's not only the time," she complained bitterly. "The work
is just too…well, it's too hard. And I'm not smart enough."

She was. But she clearly didn't believe it.

"I think the best thing at the moment is for you to—"

"Hey, Sarge!" called Dylan as he popped his head around
the door. "There's a lady here to see you."

A lady? He looked toward Emily. "Keep studying. I'll be
back in a minute and we'll continue this discussion."

"But I—"

"Hit the books," he said and smiled, then turned on his
heel.

The second floor of the surf club had recently undergone
a complete renovation following a fire four months earlier.
Now it was used for Tai Chi classes, the Big Brother program
and a couple of other local community events. Today it was a
place for Emily to study without interruption while he spent
time with Dylan.

Cameron headed down the stairs and came to an abrupt
halt when he reached the bottom tread.

*Grace.*

A jolt hit him behind the ribs. He looked at Dylan, who was
hanging off to her left and grinning. "Go and get the fishing
gear ready," he instructed and tossed him the keys to his car.

Dylan caught the keys and took off quickly. When he was
out of sight Cameron turned his attention to Grace. "Hi."

"Hello."

"You came."

She shrugged a little. "I was walking…I simply happened to… Well, I was nearby and thought I'd come in."

The sensation in his chest amplified. "I'm glad you did." Cameron held out his hand. "Come on up."

She looked at his hand and hesitated. He waited. Grace never acted on impulse. Her actions were always measured. Always in control. She looked immaculate, as usual. Her dark hair was pulled back tightly and caught in a band at her nape. The only anomaly in her seriously fashionable look was the well-worn hot pink visor on her head. She finally took his hand and he instinctively curled his fingers around hers. She didn't resist and followed him up the stairway.

When they reached the landing she withdrew her hand and crossed her arms. "So, what did you want to show me?"

Cameron smiled. "Nothing sinister."

"Not that I'm likely to believe you," she said, raising her perfectly sculpted brows.

He cracked another smile. "Come on, there's someone I'd like you to meet."

Cameron opened the door to one of the two upstairs rooms and beckoned her inside. She tagged after him and he closed the door. Emily looked up from her spot at the desk positioned by the long row of windows. He ushered Grace across the room.

"Emily, this is Grace Preston, a friend of mine."

"Girlfriend?" the teen asked and stood.

"Friend," Grace corrected as she shook Emily's hand. "And I think I just met your brother?"

"Yeah, Dylan," Emily said and laughed. "We look alike."

The toddler in the corner tapped loudly on the plastic drum he was playing with.

"And that's Riley," Cameron explained. "Emily's son."

Grace nodded, frowning a little. He could see her looking at Emily with interest before she glanced at the books on the table. "But it looks as though I'm interrupting you."

"No, you're saving me," Emily replied with a wry grin. "Sergeant Jakowski is a slave driver."

Grace laughed and the sound hit Cameron directly behind the ribs. *Damn.* He wished everything about her didn't affect him like he was a pining schoolboy. "Emily needs to study for a makeup exam in two weeks. This is a quiet place for her to hit the books while Dylan and I go fishing."

"Then I am interrupting you," Grace replied. "I should go."

"No," Cameron said, too quickly. "Stay for a while." He saw her surprised look and fought the color creeping up his neck. But she was here. And he wanted her to stay. "You're handy with the books, right?" he asked and smiled as he pulled out a chair.

Handy with the books was an understatement. Grace was the smartest person he'd ever known. As a child she'd always been top of her class, even before she'd gone to that fancy school. Then she'd headed off to New York to study finance and business. After that he'd heard she'd been headhunted by some of the top brokerage firms in the city.

Grace nodded, clearly still hesitant. "I'm not sure I can—"

"That would be great," Emily said with more enthusiasm than he'd heard from her all afternoon. "I need all the help I can get."

Cameron tapped the back of the chair and spoke. "I'll be back in a little while."

Once Cameron left, Grace sat down. Emily stared at her and grinned.

"So, are you and the Sarge—"

"No," Grace replied quickly and pushed back the heat in

her cheeks. "We're just friends," she said, even if it wasn't exactly true. "We've known one another since we were kids."

*And he was the first man I kissed.*

Even though she'd developed a silly crush on him when she was twelve, Grace knew she was a "late bloomer" when it had come to boys and sex. While her classmates were pining over pop icons and movie stars, she had her head firmly placed in textbooks or a Jane Austen novel. Being a year younger hadn't helped. She was teased for her bookish ways, her flat chest and seeming lack of interest in any of the boys from the nearby all-male college. By the time her chest arrived she'd already earned the reputation as being stuck-up and closed off from the other girls in her class. And after a while she learned to embrace the isolation from her peers. Making friends lost any appeal and she didn't waste time thinking about boys or romance.

Until the night of her sixteenth birthday.

"That explains why you don't look like his usual type," Emily said and jerked her back to the present. "I mean, they are Gucci jeans you're wearing, right?"

Grace shifted in her seat and took off her visor. She didn't like the idea of Cameron having a *type*. "You know fashion?"

Emily nodded. "I *love* fashion. Not that I can afford anything better than chain-store clothes these days. Riley keeps growing out of his gear quicker than I can buy them. But I would love to have my own store one day. And maybe study design."

Grace pressed her hair back and looked at the textbook on the table. "That's a great ambition. Now, about this makeup exam?"

Emily rolled her eyes. "I've missed a lot of school this year. Nan was helping out with Riley until my half brother and sister came to live with us." The teenager pushed the book toward Grace. "My mother is a screwup. She's in jail.

Her husband died last year. No one knows what happened to *my* dad."

Grace hid her surprise. Teenagers with serious family issues weren't something she had experience dealing with. Unlike Cameron, who she knew spent a lot of time with needy kids like Dylan and Emily. "I'm sorry."

Emily shrugged. "It happens. We're lucky we've got Nan. But she's getting old, you know, and can't do things like she used to. Besides, I have to think about Riley."

Grace glanced at the toddler, still happily playing in the corner. Adolescence, high school exams and a baby? It seemed like a heavy load. "Which is why Cameron wants you to finish high school?"

"Yeah—so I can get a good job or go to college. He's cool, you know…he just nags me a bit sometimes."

Grace smiled. "Well, nagging can be helpful."

Emily laughed. "That's what my nan says. And I guess I know that."

"But?"

The teen shrugged again. "The studying is hard. And I get so tired of being treated differently at school because I've got Riley."

Grace felt the frustration and pain in the girl's voice. She knew firsthand how it felt to be different and then ostracized. "So, how about you show me what you need to study and maybe I can help."

"Are you a teacher?"

"Finance broker."

Emily frowned. "Which means?"

"Which means I'm good with numbers," Grace replied with a wry smile.

She spent the next hour working with Emily. By the time Cameron and Dylan returned, the books were packed away and Riley was asleep in his mother's arms. Emily had asked

Grace to hold the little boy, but she'd resisted. Babies weren't her thing. Making money and math and meetings and work lunches were what she was good at.

*Not babies.*

Grace didn't have a ticking biological clock. She didn't have some deep-rooted and instinctive yearning to reproduce. She had her career. And it had always been enough.

Being back in Crystal Point wasn't going to change that. Being around Cameron wasn't going to change that either.

"I'll just drop them home," Cameron said as they watched Emily collect her knapsack and haul Riley higher in her arms.

"I should get back to the B and B and—"

"I'll be ten minutes, tops," he said. "Wait here."

Before she had a chance to object, Emily and Dylan waved goodbye and they all disappeared through the doorway. Grace lingered by the desk for a few minutes and got herself all worked up about his high-handed demands. She was just about to head home in protest when her cell rang. It was her boss, Jennifer Mullin-Shaw.

"So, are you relaxing?" Jennifer asked.

Grace was pleased the other woman couldn't see her frown. "Of course."

"And taking the therapist's advice?"

"All of it," Grace assured her. "I'm even watching old movies on cable to relax."

Jennifer laughed and they chatted for a few minutes about mundane things such as the weather and then she gave a brief rundown of her sister's wedding. Minus the part about making out with Cameron on the beach in the moonlight.

"So, you're not dwelling on what happened?"

Grace gripped the phone harder and told a tiny lie. "I haven't thought about the accident at all. I'm feeling...better."

"That's good. I'm pleased you're taking it easy. Give me a call when you're ready to come back to work."

*I'm ready now.*

But she didn't say it. Instead she ended the call and slipped the cell in her jeans pocket. Her plan to return to the B and B was forgotten when she turned on her heels and discovered Cameron standing in the doorway, arms crossed over his chest, one shoulder propped against the doorjamb.

He looked her over in that slow, infuriating way she was accustomed to. "So, how did it go with Emily?"

She nodded and placed the visor back on her head. "Good. She's a smart girl."

"Yes, she is. Did she tell you about her home life?"

"A little. She told me about her mother and how her two half siblings now live with them and her grandmother."

"Pat took the kids in when her daughter got locked up. Drugs," he explained. "It's been tough for the family. Emily and Dylan's father disappeared years ago and they've lived with their grandmother most of their lives. The father of the two younger kids was killed a few months back. But now they have a chance to start fresh with a new home out near Burdon Creek." He told her how the town had rallied to help the family purchase the small farm.

Grace thought about what he was doing for Emily's family. She tried to think of one selfless thing she done the past year and came up with nothing.

*No wonder he thinks I'm shallow. Not that I care one hoot what Cameron Jakowski thinks of me.*

"It's good of you to look out for them," she said in a vague way she suspected sounded like some weak attempt to make conversation.

"Someone has to."

*Knight in shining armor. Hero cop. All-around good guy. Not the guy for me.*

Where did that come from? Grace crossed her arms and

stared out of the window. *Those mindless minutes on the beach the night before, that's where.*

She pulled on her good sense, determined to not think about his arms, his kisses, or anything else to do with the one person who'd managed to get under her skin and make her feel like she was the most self-absorbed woman on the planet. She'd never really cared what Erik thought of her. Or Dennis. Perhaps because she'd always held herself apart and avoided getting too close. But Cameron...he was different. He saw her. Every flaw.

"So, you said you had something to show me?" she asked.

"I did?"

"Mmm-hmm," she replied and tried to dismiss the silly way her pulse raced. But he was hard to ignore in low-rise jeans and a pale blue T-shirt that showed the broadness of his chest and shoulders. And suddenly the air in the room grew hotter, thicker, like a tempting force had swept between them. She'd felt it before and always managed to ignore it. But today she couldn't. He had good looks and charm in bucket loads.

"It's nothing."

She turned her head to glance at him. "Did you get me here under false pretenses?"

"Maybe."

Warmth pushed through her blood. "And now that you have me here, what are your intentions?"

He laughed. "Ah, Grace, you are a confusing and beautiful contradiction."

The compliment part didn't help her determination to not be aware of him. "Then maybe I should leave and put you out of your misery."

"What fun would that be?"

"Who needs fun?" she shot back and managed a tight smile.

"All work and no play, Grace? How's that worked out for you so far?"

"Well enough," she replied.

"Liar," he said softly. "And if I come a little closer you'll be shaking in those three-hundred-dollar shoes of yours."

She drew in a breath. "You really do overstate your charm. If I'm shaking, it's with disbelief that you're so egotistical."

He chuckled and perched his behind on the desk. "You know, Grace, I like you this way...fired up and ready for anything."

Grace raised one brow. "Well, get used to it."

"Don't get me wrong," he said and crossed his arms. "I also like the woman you were last night."

Heat crept up her neck. "Well, don't get too used to *that*."

He laughed and then just as quickly looked serious. "So, tell me about the accident?" He'd heard that part of her conversation with Jennifer? Damn. *Deny everything*.

"It's nothing."

He shook his head. "I don't believe you. I know there's something wrong with you, Grace. I also know you're too proud, or too stubborn, to say what it is because you think it will give me some kind of ridiculous advantage. Tell me," he insisted as his brown-eyed gaze scanned her face. "What accident were you talking about just now?"

She drew in a breath and the truth felt heavy across her shoulders. Grace closed her eyes for a moment. Images jumbled in her head. Lights flashing, brakes screeching, metal crunching...it was over in a flash of a second. And then there had been an eerie quiet, followed by the sound of her own terrified breath.

And suddenly she wanted to tell him everything.

"I was in a crash," she explained quietly, feeling raw and exposed and more alone than she'd ever dare admit. "I was in a car crash."

Cameron responded quickly. "What? When?"

"A couple of months ago."

"Were you hurt?"

She shrugged. Her scars were emotional, not physical. "I dislocated my shoulder and had a few cuts and abrasions. Nothing serious."

Cameron's gaze was unwavering. "It wasn't just a fender bender, though, was it?"

"No."

"It was a serious crash?"

She shuddered. "Yes."

"And you haven't told your family about it, have you?"

"No."

He pushed himself off the table. "Why not?"

Grace's throat tightened. She hadn't spoken of the accident with anyone other than her boss and her therapist. Her work colleagues had stayed off the topic, even when she'd arrived at the office after taking a week off. They knew she didn't do deep and meaningful discussions. They knew she didn't want to talk about Richard's death. "There was no point."

He shook his head. "No point? They're your *family*. You were hurt, Grace, don't you think they had a right to know?"

The heaviness in her throat increased. "I wasn't hurt badly," she said in a defensive tone. *Not like Richard.* "It wasn't worth making people worry."

He frowned. "People? I'm not talking about random strangers, Grace," he said and grabbed her hand. "I'm talking about your family. Your parents. Your brother and sisters."

She tried to pull away put he held her firm. "You don't understand. I can't be like that. I can't let out every emotion I have. I don't have what it takes to…to…"

"To what?" he encouraged so gently the heat in her throat turned into an all-out burn. "To get close to someone?" he asked.

Grace nodded.

He urged her toward him and she jerked as her body pressed against his. "And yet," he said as he curled one arm around her waist. "You feel close now."

Her emotions heaved. "Please don't…don't tease me."

"I'm not teasing," he said so gently her insides contracted. "I promise. But it might help to talk about it."

Grace didn't want his help. She wanted to run back to the B & B. But she didn't move. And instead, she spoke a truth she hadn't shared with anyone. "Okay…here's the truth. After the crash I had a…meltdown," she admitted. "My boss made me come home. It wasn't my choice. I wanted to work through it in New York. I didn't want to come back here. I didn't want sympathy or pity. I didn't want to feel *anything*."

He looked into her eyes. "Does feeling scare you that much, Grace?"

It scared her. It terrified her. If she let herself really *feel* then she would be exposed…vulnerable. *Weak.* "Yes."

He touched her face. "Then I think you're exactly where you need to be."

In his arms? It was the one place she could never be. She shook her head and pulled away. "Promise me you won't say anything. I don't want my parents to—"

"I promise," he said gently and dropped his arms. "For now."

# Chapter Four

Later that afternoon Cameron lingered by the table in his mother's kitchen while she stacked plastic containers into two separate carry bags.

"You know, I can cook for myself," he mentioned, and grinned.

"Me, too," his sister Lauren piped up in agreement.

Irene Jakowski gave a look which said she didn't believe either of them. "Humor me and take this anyway."

Which is exactly what they would do. He inhaled the delicious scent of the cabbage rolls. He did love his mother's *golabki*.

"Not too much, please, *Matka*," Lauren patted her flat stomach and used the Polish word for *mother,* which his parents preferred. "Or I'll end up as big as a house."

"Beef and a little mushroom wrapped in cabbage leaves won't add any pounds," Irene said and raised her brows at her youngest child. "Besides, you're too skinny."

rue," Cameron agreed and winced when Lauren's elbow jabbed him in the ribs.

But he was right. His sister looked too thin. Which wasn't a surprise, considering she'd endured a messy divorce a year earlier. He was pleased she now seemed to be pulling through the worst of it.

"The wedding was just lovely, don't you think?" Irene looked at Cameron as she spoke. He knew where it was going. "Evie made a lovely bride."

He was pretty sure Irene had once hoped he'd hook up with Evie, but he'd never felt that way about her. Grace, on the other hand…his mother knew a little of their failed relationship. It wasn't something he enjoyed mulling over.

"The dress looked fabulous," Lauren chimed in to say. His sister and mother owned a bridal store in Bellandale and he knew they'd fitted Evie for her gown. "I knew the off-the-shoulder design was a good—"

Cameron groaned. "If you two are gonna talk dresses I'm outta here."

His mother chuckled. "I only said she made a lovely bride. But all the Preston girls are quite lovely, aren't they? Even Grace, once you get past her prickles."

"Prickles?" Lauren echoed with a frown. "You mean icy barbs. There's no doubt she's beautiful, but she doesn't exactly bring on the warm fuzzies. Not like Evie and M.J." Lauren grabbed the bag their mother passed her way. "Anyway, enough gossiping, I have to get going."

Lauren hugged them both and was gone within a minute.

"I should get going, too," he said, grabbing his keys from the table.

"Your dad won't be back from golf for another hour," she said and grabbed the kettle. "Feel like staying for coffee?"

He glanced at his watch. "Sure."

"Do you also feel like talking about whatever's on your mind at the moment?"

He had to hand it to his mother—she had the female intuition thing down pat. "Not especially."

"Grace, I suppose?"

He looked up. "What?"

"You're always edgy when she's in town. I saw you talking to her at the wedding so I figured there was some connection to your current mood."

Cameron pulled out a chair and sat down. "You're imagining things. And my mood is fine."

Irene shrugged. "How long is she back for this time?"

"I'm not sure."

"Barbara is worried about her," his mother confided. Barbara Preston was Irene's closest friend. "Know anything?"

Cameron ignored the tightness in his chest. He didn't like lying but wasn't about to get drawn into a conversation about Grace, especially when he'd promised to keep her secrets. "Not a thing."

Irene nodded, gave a wry smile and then switched the subject. "So, you're coming to the reunion this year?"

The Jakowski family reunion was an annual event that had been tradition for more than thirty years. "I'll do my best."

"It will make your father happy if you come."

"I know," he said, but doubted he'd attend. He'd missed four of the past five years and this year was shaping up to be no exception. Because even though Franciszek Jakowski treated him like he was his son in every possible way and he loved the other man dearly, when it came to the huge family gathering, Cameron always felt like a fraud.

His mother had married Franciszek when she was just twenty with a three-year-old on her hip. By the time Lauren arrived a few years later he had already been adopted by Franciszek and he was the only father Cameron knew. His

...ical father had bailed well before he was born, not pre-
...d for teenage parenthood. Irene never talked about him
and Cameron never asked. It was only sometimes that he
wondered about him, or when faced with the reunion picnic
that he felt like he was there by default. Because Jakowski
blood didn't run through his veins. He wasn't really part of
the four generations of Polish ancestry that was celebrated by
his parents and grandparents and uncle and aunts and countless cousins. He was the biological son of a seventeen-year-
old misfit who had disappeared off the radar once his teenage
girlfriend discovered she was pregnant.

"Please try," he heard his mother say and it quickly got his
thoughts back on track.

He drank some of the coffee she'd placed in front of him
and smiled. "I will, *Matka,* I promise."

A few hours later he was sitting on the wide timber deck
of his double story, four bedroom, two living rooms, way too
big to be practical house, a drink in front of him that he hadn't
touched. He'd purchased the half-acre block nine years ago
and then designed and built the home, of which he only used
about one quarter of the rooms.

It was cold out and he heard the sea crashing against the
rocks. In the distance he could see the lights from a vessel
in the shipping lane, most likely a tanker on its way to collect cargo from the port south of Bellandale. Locally grown
sugar cane was shipped out by the ton and the big ships came
by weekly during crushing season.

Cattle bellowed in the distance and the sound was oddly
comforting. Living in the most northern end of Crystal Point,
he had only one close neighbor—an elderly couple who lived
in a small house across from his in the quiet cul-de-sac. Cameron liked the solitude and the view. With hundreds of acres
of unspoiled pasture behind and the Pacific Ocean to the
front, it was an idyllic location.

The dog at his feet yawned and rolled onto its back and it made him smile a bit. The big, goofy mutt had a way of doing that. But the smile on his face didn't last long. His thoughts were full of Grace.

She'd been in a car crash? She could have died.

*Life without Grace in it...*

The idea made his bones ache. In just twenty-four hours she'd gotten so deep under his skin he could barely think about anything else. He wanted to call her, hear her voice. He stared at the telephone, then grabbed it and his drink and headed inside. Jed hunkered after him and when Cameron started flicking off lights the dog settled on his big mat by the back door.

Once the house was locked up he took a shower and then dropped into bed. The digital clock on the side table blinked ten-thirty at him. Late enough to sleep, he figured and switched off the lamp before he rolled onto his stomach.

Green eyes haunted him instantly.

He grabbed a pillow and punched it a couple of times.

*Green eyes and perfectly straight almost black hair.*

Cameron flipped onto his back with a groan, determined to not think about her, and failed miserably. Her unexpected vulnerability distracted him, made him forget she was the world's number one ice princess. He shouldn't want her. But he did.

She made him crazy. Still.

*And her kisses were like something from out of this world....*

The first time he'd kissed her was on her sixteenth birthday. He'd deliberately arrived late to her party to avoid his growing awareness of her whenever she came near. She was too young. Noah's—his best friend's—sister. And despite the odd time he'd catch her watching him when she thought he wasn't looking, she'd barely give him the time of day. Until that night. A darkened doorway and the heady beat of some old song in the background had shifted her usual reserve. A few minutes alone and the temptation of a birthday kiss and he couldn't help but claim her lips. If it hadn't been for a strict voice in his head telling him she was off-limits for at least a couple more years, they might have done more than share a sweet, unforgettable kiss.

A year and a half later he asked her out for real. By then she'd finished school and he was settled into his career as a second-year officer, had wheels and was saving to buy some land where he'd eventually build a house he hoped she'd one day be proud to live in. He'd had plans, ideas, and every one had included Grace Preston. But three months into their relationship she'd said goodbye and headed to New York.

*So what the hell am I thinking? Like I want to be on the receiving end of her rejection again.*

Was it just sexual frustration that had him feeling like he did? He flipped back onto his stomach. If he kept thinking about how it felt to kiss her, touch her, stroke her beautiful skin, he'd never get to sleep.

Too late.

Cameron rolled again and stared at the ceiling.

He closed his eyes. A busy week loomed ahead. He had a pile of work on his desk, including a few court appearances. One to give evidence against a repeat DUI offender looking to avoid jail time and Cameron doubted the hard-line magistrate would be lenient. The other two involved breaches of domestic violence orders.

He took a deep breath and tried to relax. But when sleep finally came, his dreams were haunted by bright green eyes...

Because she prided herself on being action oriented, Grace had spent most of the afternoon and evening coming up with ways to pull herself from the uncharacteristic funk that had taken hold of her life.

And one thought kept coming back to her.

*Cameron.*

If he dared breathe a word to her family she would be completely outed.

And one thing Grace knew for certain—once they knew what had happened to her she would be enveloped in their care and compassion and her fraught nerves would surely fracture. She also knew she didn't have the strength for it. It was easier to stay stoic and in control. Easier to act the role she'd played all her life—the supercool and tough-as-nails Grace who would return to New York without anyone guessing she was broken inside.

All she had to do was make sure Cameron kept his mouth shut.

Grace called him again the following morning and when the call went to voice mail, decided to take more action and see him in person. She took Evie's Honda and drove past his house and since his car wasn't there, figured he was at work. So she headed into town.

The police station was easy to find and she scored a parking spot outside. She'd dressed in a black skirt, matching jacket and collared red shirt. The black knee-high boots and patent bag added to the effect she wanted. All business. All control.

When she reached the reception desk, Grace took a deep breath and spoke to the young woman behind the counter. "I'd like to see Sergeant Jakowski."

"Do you have an appointment?"

"No. But I'd appreciate it if you told him I was here."

One name given, a telephone call and a few minutes wait and she had what she wanted. She took the lift to the second level and when she stepped out into the hall found him waiting.

"This is a surprise."

Grace shrugged as she walked toward him. "I called your cell but you didn't pick up."

"So you decided to start stalking me."

She stilled about five feet from him and waited until two uniformed officers passed before responding. "Yes, you look like you're shaking in your boots."

He smiled. "Speaking of boots," he said and looked her over. "They do the job."

"And what job is that?"

"The job of distracting me enough so you can get your own way."

He liked her boots? "You think I'm that manipulative?" she inquired and stopped in front of him.

Cameron opened a door to his left. "I think you're a woman who wants something."

She did. His silence.

"I just came to talk."

He ushered her into the room and closed the door. "So, talk."

Grace looked at him. He filled out his uniform in a way that got her attention. The pale blue shirt fit him perfectly, highlighting his broad shoulders and lean waist. She quickly ignored her wavering thoughts. "I wanted to know if you'll stand by your promise to keep my private business private."

He came toward the desk and sat on the edge. "I'm not about to be a buffer between you and your family," he said with a kind of irritated disbelief. "They're your *family,* Grace. I don't understand your reluctance to tell them about your accident."

"No, you wouldn't," she shot back. "But it's my decision to make."

He crossed his arms. "It's not hard to let people in."

"Now you sound like my therapist," she said and let out a heavy sigh.

"You're seeing a shrink?"

"Counselor," she corrected and quickly realized she'd said too much. "Because the accident was work-related the company was obliged to supply grief counseling to—"

"Whoa," Cameron held up a hand. "Back up a minute. You're seeing a *grief* counselor. Explain that to me."

Grace's skin prickled. "It's normal in these circumstances."

"What circumstances?"

She drew in a breath, steadying herself. "When someone has died."

He took a second to respond. "Someone died? Who?"

"Richard Bennett," she said quietly and felt the intensity of his stare through to her blood. "A work colleague. We were traveling together at the time of the accident."

"Was anyone else in the car?"

"No," she replied. "Richard was driving. We were on our way to meet with a client. But we crashed. It was no one's fault."

"So he died. And you survived?"

She nodded. Her counselor had explained survivor's guilt several times. She'd brushed it off. Ignored it. "The therapist thought I should come home and be with my family for a while. My boss agreed."

"That sounds like good advice."

Grace shrugged. "But unnecessary. I have a job that I'm good at and a life in New York that suits me. I didn't see the need to change that."

"Obviously the people around you did. What about your friends in New York?"

She shrugged again. There were acquaintances and work colleagues. But friends? None who she was close to. The only person who'd visited her after the accident had been her boss, Jennifer. "You know me."

He looked at her for the longest time before he spoke again.

"I do," he said quietly. "And I know your family. They're kind, good people who care about you."

"Precisely why I don't want to alarm them."

"Nice try. What's the real reason?"

Grace got to her feet. "That is the reason. Does it seem impossible that I don't want to worry them? And it's not like I was seriously hurt. I'm fine. Just fine."

His brows came up and he stood and rocked back a little on his heels. "You're a lot of things, Grace…but I suspect *fine* isn't one of them."

Her annoyance spiked. "You don't know anything about it, so I'd rather you didn't try to psychoanalyze me. All I want is your word that you won't say anything to my family, particularly my parents. I'll tell them when I'm ready, and not before."

"You know, I don't think I quite believe you. You're obviously in denial about an incredibly traumatic experience. The best thing you could do is come clean and talk about it."

What a self-righteous jerk. He knew nothing about what was best for her.

"So you won't keep your word, is that what you're saying?"

He rubbed his chin. "I'm not sure keeping my word would be what's best for you."

She clutched her handbag to her side. "Since it's obvious you don't have the decency to respect my wishes and seem to think you have the right to an opinion about my life, I intend to keep as far away from you as possible while I'm back in Crystal Point." She drew in a deep breath. "Or to put it another way—go to hell, Jakowski!"

Then she was out the door and down the corridor as quickly as her feet could carry her.

Of course, in a town as small as Crystal Point, staying away from Cameron was almost impossible.

When she pulled into the driveway in front of her brother's home that evening and saw Cameron's electric-blue sedan parked there, she immediately considered bailing. But she wouldn't have been able to explain that to Noah. Her brother had dropped by the B and B that afternoon to repair a window lock and had invited her to share dinner with his family. Since she still had one guest to attend to, Grace declined dinner and agreed to a coffee visit instead.

Only she hadn't anticipated seeing the one person she wanted to avoid.

She wondered if he'd wrangled an invitation just to irritate her or dropped in without one. It was her sister-in-law who answered the door and invited her inside.

"We've just finished dinner," Callie said as she closed the door. "But I can get you something if you—"

"Oh, I'm fine," Grace assured her. "I've already eaten."

Her brother and Cameron were in the living room. "Grace," Noah said and came around the sofa. He kissed her cheek. He knew she wasn't the hugging type. "Great to see you. Everything okay?"

"Yes." She glanced at Cameron, who was sitting on the sofa. In jeans and T-shirt he looked relaxed and handsome and possessed such an easygoing manner that when he smiled Grace couldn't help but smile back. *Stay on track.* She rattled the bag she carried. "I brought something for the children, I hope you don't mind?"

Noah grinned. "Not at all. I'll round them up."

Her brother left the room and once Callie disappeared to make coffee, Grace glared at him. "What are you doing here?"

"I was invited," Cameron said, smiling as he looked at the bag she carried. "Gifts are a nice touch. I trust you remember the kids' names?"

She frowned. "I'm not that out of the loop. I am their aunt, you know."

"Nice outfit, by the way," he said of her long denim skirt and pale green sweater.

"Spare me the compliments."

He chuckled. "Very…aunt appropriate."

"Are you suggesting I look like a spinster aunt now?"

He laughed again. "Hardly. There's nothing the least bit spinsterish about you, Grace."

"Other than the fact I'm not married?"

"You've still got time to change that."

Grace shook her head slowly. She didn't want to talk about marriage with him. Because despite the denials she knew would come, being around him made her think, imagine. And those kinds of thoughts were pointless. She had her life—it was set. "Marriage is not in my plans. A husband and kids wouldn't mix with my work."

"And you wouldn't consider giving up your career?"

She placed her handbag by the fireplace and didn't quite have the courage to meet his gaze until she'd inhaled a steadying breath. "My career comes first. I'm not the marriage-and-babies sort. I'll leave that to women like Evie and Callie."

He looked at her oddly. "You don't think a woman can have both?"

She raised her shoulders a little. "I've worked with a few women trying to juggle career and family and they always complained how difficult it was. Better to do one, and do it well, than try to divide the time and become mediocre at both."

"That's a rather dim view of things," he said. "What happens when you fall in love?"

"I won't," she said quickly and tried to breathe through the heat rising up her collarbone. "I mean, I've never felt that. I'm not sure I believe it exists."

"I'm sure your brother and Callie would disagree. And

Evie and Scott. Your parents have had a happy marriage, right? Mine, too."

Grace managed a tight smile. "And yet you've managed to avoid it yourself?"

"But I believe in marriage," he said and rested an arm along the back of the sofa.

"Oh, I thought you were too busy carving notches into your bedpost."

He smiled in that sexy way and Grace harnessed all her resistance. "The fact you've been thinking about my bed leads me to believe there's hope for you yet, *Princess*."

"I don't know what—"

"Here we are!" Noah said as the kids rushed into the room. The twins, five-year-old Hayley and Matthew, raced toward her, while nine-year-old Jamie trailed behind. Noah's youngest daughter wasn't a child to be held back and she insisted on hugging Grace and then demanded to know what was in the bag. Grace spread the gifts around and made certain Jamie received his while the twins tore at wrapping paper. The books and DVDs were a clear winner. Once they'd said thank-you, the kids quickly disappeared to their rooms.

"Where's Lily?" she asked of Noah's teenage daughter.

"Studying at a friend's," Callie said as she came back into the room carrying a tray.

Grace shook the bag. "I'll leave this for her."

"It's lovely of you to think about the kids like this," Callie said and passed mugs around.

Grace glanced toward Cameron, and then quickly focused her thoughts. Chalk one up for the closed-off aunt. "My pleasure. I don't get to see them often enough."

"We don't see you enough either," Noah said as he took a spot on the other sofa and suggested she sit down.

She made her way around the sofa and sat beside Cameron. He didn't move and his hand rested only an inch from her shoulder. But she could *feel* him. The connection and awareness was like nothing she'd ever experienced. Grace gripped her mug and drank the coffee. Noah watched her, Callie smiled and Cameron's silence was suddenly deafening.

When he finally spoke she jumped a little. "So, Grace was telling me she'll watch the kids for you next Tuesday."

*I was?*

Noah looked surprised. "Really?"

"I think that would be great," Callie said and squeezed her husband's knee. "Your parents offered—but I know they'd like to be at the awards dinner."

Awards dinner? She looked at Cameron. There was laughter and direct challenge in his eyes. *Damn his sexy hide.* He was deliberately trying to antagonize her. She managed a tight smile. "I'm more than happy to watch them."

"It's only the twins," Callie explained. "Jamie and Lily want to be there to see their dad get his award."

She feigned knowledge, knew that Cameron was laughing to himself and made a point to settle this particular score with him when they were alone. "What time do you want me here?"

"Six o'clock," Noah said.

They chatted for another twenty minutes and she was grateful her brother didn't question her about New York or how long she intended to stay in Crystal Point. Finally, Cameron got up to leave, said goodbye and offered to walk her out.

Once they were by their cars and out of earshot she glared at him. "What was that about?" she demanded. "Has meddling in my life suddenly become an entertaining pastime for you?"

"More of an *interesting* pastime," he corrected with a self-indulgent grin.

"And clearly volunteering me to babysit is your idea of a joke?"

"Well, you did say your therapist suggested you spend time with your family."

She wanted to slug his smug face. Instead, she drew in a steadying breath. "Thank you for your charitable concern. However, I can arrange my own family time without your interference."

He grinned. "Really? And did you know about your brother's award?"

"Of course," she fibbed.

His brow came up. "Well, in case it slipped your mind, it's a community award. And a big deal. Preston Marine offers traineeships for young people with disabilities. The award is recognition of his work helping these kids."

She knew her brother did that, didn't she? Noah had been at the helm of the boat-building business that had been started by her grandfather for over a decade. Her father had retired a couple of years earlier. A niggling shame seared between her shoulder blades. Was she so busy with her own problems she'd forgotten everything about where she came from?

"Of course," she said again and knew he wasn't convinced.

He came a little closer. "On the other hand, if you don't think you're up to the task of watching the kids, I'm sure they could find someone else."

Grace bristled. "No need for that," she assured him and continued to fight the urge to slap his handsome face. "I'm quite confident I'll manage the task."

He laughed out loud. "Well, that's great to hear, *Princess*. Because the price for my silence has just gone up."

Her blood stilled. "What does that mean?"

"Emily needs a tutor for the next two weeks."

A tutor? "I can't possibly—"

"No lessons," he said, cutting her off. "No silence."

Shock leached the color from her face. "That's blackmail."

"Friendly incentive," he said and grinned. "Besides, Emily likes you."

In truth she liked Emily, too, and even though part of her sensed she would be able to help the teenager, Grace wasn't about to be railroaded. "I'm not qualified to do that."

"You're perfectly qualified," he said and moved closer to open her driver's door.

"I won't do it."

"Sure you will. You fight a good fight, Grace," he said with a kind of arrogant overconfidence. "But not good enough. I'll make sure Pat drops Emily off at Dunn Inn around four tomorrow for her lesson. Good night."

He was close enough that for a second she thought he might kiss her. For a second she actually wanted him to.

But he didn't.

She got into the car and drove off and wondered what had happened to the well-ordered, organized life she'd once had. The life that had been about clients and meetings and skipped lunches and business dinners. Not about tutoring teenage girls, babysitting five-year-olds and dreaming about kissing Cameron Jakowski.

And then, she wondered how she was supposed to want that old life back once she returned to New York.

Cameron stayed away from Grace for the following two days. Mostly because he knew it would drive her crazy. Being the rigid control freak she was, he'd bet his boots she'd want to wail at him some more about being pushed into tutoring Emily. So he gave her a couple of days to work with the teenager without him hovering.

He arrived at Dunn Inn late Wednesday afternoon and found Grace in the downstairs kitchen, preparing things for the evening meal. Of course she could cook. There were a couple of unfamiliar vehicles parked in the circular driveway, indicating guests were in residence. Even working over a stove she was immaculate. Black pants and white shirt and a pristine apron he figured probably wouldn't dare crease, made her look formidable and beautiful.

He remained beneath the threshold and watched her work for a moment.

When she finally looked up and let out a small, surprised gasp, he spoke. "How's the tutoring going?"

"I'm holding up my end of the bargain," she replied and placed a lid on a saucepan. "Emily's a smart girl and I think she'll ace the test with a little more studying."

He walked into the room. "I think so, too."

She frowned. "Is her son's father in the picture? I don't want to ask her directly if the subject is off-limits."

Cameron shrugged. "He took off when Riley was born."

She stayed silent for a moment, looking at him. "Is that why you…"

"Is that why I…what?" he prompted. But he knew what she was thinking. His own parentage wasn't exactly a state secret. Barbara Preston had introduced his mother to Franciszek all those years ago, so they were well aware he was adopted by his dad.

"Nothing," she said tightly and pulled a frying pan off an overhead hook.

"Do you think I'm trying to get over my abandonment issues by helping Emily and Riley?"

"I…don't…know," she said and he noticed she looked a little paler than usual. Maybe she wasn't sleeping? Well, she wasn't the only one. "Are you?"

"I never knew my biological father," he said quietly. "So there's no real issue to get past."

One brow rose. "You don't miss what you've never had, you mean?"

"Exactly. And I help kids like Emily and Dylan because

it needs to be done. Otherwise they could fall through the cracks in social services."

She untied the apron. "I don't know how you manage it, but you always make me feel…feel…"

"Feel what?"

"Self-centered," she said and tossed the apron on the bench. "Selfish. Shallow. Superficial."

At least he was making her feel something. That was a start, right? "Success and beauty don't go hand in hand with being superficial."

She stared at him and the mood between them quickly shifted. His attraction to her had a will of its own and air was suddenly charged with awareness. Her hair was pulled back in a tight ponytail and he had the urge to set it free. Memories of kissing her on the beach only a few nights before rushed back and filled his blood. Her icy reserve had slipped and she'd kissed him back passionately. And he wanted to feel that passion again.

"Don't."

Cameron tilted his head. "Don't what?"

"Don't say I'm…you know."

"Beautiful?" He laughed softly. "No point denying the obvious."

"Like it's all I am."

Cameron moved around the counter. "That's not what I said. But I guess it's easier to think the worst of me."

She turned to face him. "Nothing is easy with you."

He reached out and touched her jaw. When she didn't move he rubbed his thumb across her cheek. "Then let's call a truce."

"A truce?"

"Yes," he said and stepped closer. "And let's stop pretending we don't want each other."

## Chapter Five

*He wants me.*

She couldn't remember the last time a man had said that to her.

Or the last time she'd wanted to hear it. Erik's lukewarm attentions hadn't bothered her because she'd felt the same way toward him. And Dennis was no different. But her feelings for Cameron were different. They always had been. They were there, under the surface, waiting to jump up and take hold. For years she'd been safe in New York—away from him and the connection that simmered between them.

She drew in a tight breath. "I don't have casual sex."

"And you think I do?" he asked and dropped his hand.

Grace raised a brow. "We've already had the conversation about your reputation."

"You shouldn't believe all you hear, Grace."

*Yes, I should.* It was safer to think of him as a woman-izer. Safer to imagine him making love to someone else. But that notion made her insides contract. *Not that I want him to make love to me.* "I've got three weeks, Cameron. And I'm not going to complicate things by...by..."

"Not everything is so black-and-white."

Grace crossed her arms. "What does that mean?"

"It means you can't put every feeling into a neat little package because you're determined to control everything. The truth is we've been dancing around this for years. I'd rather it be out there and on the table."

She pushed back her shoulders. "I wouldn't. We have a deal—and that's all we have. I want your silence and I'll tutor Emily in return."

He blatantly ignored her. "You haven't got anyone staying here after tomorrow, right?"

"Right," she replied suspiciously. "The place is empty until after Scott and Evie return the weekend after next."

"Good. Pat is taking the kids out to the farm in Burdon Creek this weekend. There's still some work to be done on the place before they can make the move permanently, so I thought you might like to help me give them a hand for a couple of days. Plus you'll get a chance to keep tutoring Emily."

*No way.* "I can't do that."

"Sure you can," he said and smiled. "It'll be good for you."

"I don't—"

"Just think of all that fresh country air," he said with one brow raised. "Wouldn't that be exactly what the doctor ordered?"

Yes, she thought, it probably would be. But it didn't mean she was about to agree. Spending the weekend with Cameron, in any circumstances, was a complication—and temptation—she didn't need.

"No," she said quietly.

He shrugged, infuriating her. "No weekend, no deal."

Grace felt her control slip away. She thought she had everything settled. A month back in Crystal Point and then she'd return to New York—that was the plan. This wasn't. "More blackmail? Forget it. I'm not spending the weekend with you."

"Emily and Riley will be there. And Pat and the kids. There'll be plenty of chaperones, Grace, so you can relax."

She didn't want a chaperone. She didn't want to relax. "I said no."

"No weekend, no deal," he said again. "Unless, of course, you would prefer to tell your family about the car accident which could have killed you and how you didn't care enough to inform them at the time."

Grace glared at him. "You're an ass, Jakowski. I *will* tell them and you'll have no hold over me."

He grabbed the cell phone on the countertop and held it toward her. "Here you go."

She froze. He knew she wouldn't take the phone. He knew she wasn't ready to tell her family what had happened. One word about the accident and she would also have to talk about her therapist, Richard and the whole awful experience. She lingered over another refusal and considered how hurt her parents would be once they found out the truth.

"Okay," she said resignedly. "I'll go with you. To help out and to tutor Emily," she said with emphasis. "And that's all."

He nodded and stepped back. "I'll pick you up Friday morning, eight o'clock."

Then he dropped the phone back on the counter and left.

The next morning Grace went shopping for new jeans and a couple of polo shirts. Bellandale had a few nice boutiques and she couldn't help splurging on a new pair of fire-engine-red heels that simply screamed "pick me." She also purchased a pair of sensible boots. They were the kind she knew people wore in the country, ankle-length with a square block heel. She walked around the B and B at night in them to try to break in the stiff leather and got mean-looking blisters on her toes as a result.

She also kept up her end of the deal and tutored Emily each afternoon.

"So, you're hanging out at the farm this weekend?" the teenager asked as they ended the lesson on Thursday evening.

Grace closed her laptop. "Yes."

Emily grinned. "Ever been on a farm before?"

"When I was young," she replied. "My grandparents had a small fruit farm and I used to visit sometimes." Not often, though. The farm was more Evie's and Noah's thing back then. Most of her vacations from boarding school were spent in Crystal Point. When her grandparents passed away the farm was sold.

Emily packed her books in her satchel. "So," she said with a curious edge. "You and Sarge—there's really nothing going on between you guys?"

"Not a thing," she said quickly and ignored her flaming cheeks. "Make sure you take your books tomorrow—we can continue with this on the weekend."

"I don't get a break?"

"No chance. One more week at this pace and you'll easily pass the exam."

Emily dropped the bag to her feet. "Not that it will do me much good. It's not like I'm going to get a great job or anything."

"It's not?"

The girl shrugged. "I've got a kid, and even with Nan's help it's gonna be hard to do what I really want to do—which is study fashion design. I work at a coffee place three mornings a week when Nan can watch him. But once she moves to the farm I won't have anyone here. It sucks, but I get why she wants to move. Dylan was getting into a lot of trouble before Sarge came along and he's really looking forward to living on the farm."

"What about day care?" Grace suggested, not really having a clue.

She shrugged again. "I can't really afford it. And I don't want to miss out on Riley growing up. But I want to go to design school, too…" She sighed heavily. "I guess it will work itself out."

Grace felt for the girl. "If design school is where you want to go, then it's exactly what you should do." She smiled gently. "You should follow your dreams, Emily."

Like she'd followed the dreams set out before her. But were they her own dreams? New York. A huge apartment. Designer clothes. A successful career. In the midst of trying to prove herself she'd gotten swept up in wanting what had been expected of her. But the truth was, none of it really satisfied her anymore. The money and fancy apartment were part of the facade that had become her life. When she was younger and ambition had burned in her, Grace hadn't noticed how alone she actually was. Perhaps her failed relationships with Dennis and Erik had amplified that feeling. Or maybe it was knowing both Noah and Evie had found their happily-ever-after that made her question what was really important. And now, more than ever, she didn't know where she belonged.

When Cameron arrived to pick her up Friday morning, Grace was waiting outside the bed-and-breakfast, her Gucci luggage at her heels. She pulled at the lapels of her soft leather jacket and ran her hands down her fine-gauge wool trousers as he eased the big, powerful blue car alongside the curb. It was cold and barely eight o'clock.

He got out and flicked open the trunk. Her heart stopped when he moved around the vehicle. Dressed in jeans and a long-sleeved gray Henley shirt, he looked so good she could barely swallow.

"Morning," he said easily.

Grace walked toward the passenger door and tried desperately to ignore her traitorous feelings. "Be careful with my cases," she demanded with a frosty glare.

He laughed. "Not a morning person, *Princess?*"

Grace opened the car and got inside. What was the worst thing that could happen? She might break a nail or get a few blisters? *I can handle that. I can handle anything.*

She took a deep breath and immediately wrinkled her nose. Something didn't smell quite right. When she heard a strange, almost guttural sound she snapped her neck around and found herself staring into a pair of piercing amber eyes and the most unattractive, jowly, drooling face she'd ever seen.

Grace's breath stopped. *Oh, my God!* The dreadful beast licked his chops and saliva leached from his pinkish, puckered mouth. She jerked her head back to the front and closed her eyes, gripping her hands together.

When Cameron got back into the car she spoke through tight lips. "There's something big and horribly smelly in the backseat."

"That's Jed," Cameron said with a laugh. He started the car and the hideous-looking animal woofed.

The sound reverberated in her eardrum like a trombone. "What is it?" she asked, trying not to think about the terrible smell racing up her nose.

"A dog. My dog."

He had a dog. The biggest, ugliest dog he could find by the looks of things. Grace's only recent experience with animals was her neighbor's Himalayan cat she sometimes watched. Noah and Callie had two dogs, but not like the thing in the backseat.

She glanced at him, determined not to look at the beast in the back. "What kind of dog?"

"Dogue de Bordeaux."

It sounded French. The only French dog she'd seen was a poodle. "It smells."

"He's not an *it*," Cameron corrected as he steered the car in an arc and down The Parade. The road ran the length of the town, a buffer between the narrow parkland and walking track along water's edge and the long row of houses, which ranged from small beach homes to some three-story mansions. "His name is Jed, like I said. And you'll get used to his breath."

"I'd rather not."

Cameron laughed again. "He's a good dog."

"Who needs a breath mint."

"Did you just make a joke, Grace?"

She pushed her handbag to the feet. "Unbelievable, I know. Imagine, me with a sense of humor."

Cameron was imagining a lot of things. Like tugging her perfectly pulled-back hair down for one. There wasn't a tendril out of place. He couldn't see her eyes shielded behind designer sunglasses and wanted to know if they were scorching through him. And the leather jacket fitted like it had been tailored for her. Nothing out of place. Immaculate and beautiful.

She looked at him. "Where exactly are we going?"

"Burdon Creek. It's three hundred and eighteen kilometers west of Bellandale and has a population of one hundred and six. One shop, which is also a gas station, a pub and a post office, and that's about it."

"And the family is happy to settle there?"

"Yes," he replied. "There's a bigger town a few miles up the road where they can get everything they need. It will be good for Dylan. He was a troubled kid when we first met. His father bailed when he was young and his mother had been in and out of drug rehab for years. His two half siblings lived with their father, but he was killed last year in an industrial accident and the kids went back to their mother and Dylan and Emily." Cameron knew how difficult it had been for Dylan to adjust to having his brother and sister living in the small house he shared with his mother, older sister and grandmother. "When his mother was arrested for possession the kids were placed in their grandmother's care. It was her third offense and she got four years' jail time."

"And the children have stayed with their grandmother?"

"Yeah. Pat's a good woman and really wants to give the kids a stable home. But the house she was in only had two small bedrooms. For the past ten months we've been raising money to pull together a deposit so she could buy a home for the kids. A few local businesses came on board and we found the place at Burdon Creek. It needed a bit of work, but most of the structural stuff has been done now. We had contractors volunteer and the past few months they've been traveling back and forth to get the place ready for Pat and the kids."

Grace flipped her sunglasses off and looked at him. "So in between my tutoring Emily what else will we be doing?"

"Painting, moving a bit of furniture, decorating...that sort of thing."

Her perfectly arched brows rose dramatically. "Decorating?"

"I thought you'd be good at it," he said.

"Why?"

He shrugged. "Because you did the decorating for Noah's showroom last year. And you always look like you've stepped off the pages of one of those glossy magazines."

Cameron looked at her and swore he saw a smile tug at the corner of her mouth.

"Is that a compliment?" she asked quietly.

"Absolutely."

"Thank you...I think." The smile grew wider. "But you should know I hired an interior decorator to do my apartment and Noah's showroom. I just supervised."

Cameron grinned. "Looks like you're in charge of moving furniture then."

She laughed delightfully and his insides crunched. It was way too easy being with her like this. He relaxed and pressed a button on the iPod in the center console. Coldplay's unique sound filled the space between them and he wondered for a moment if she'd prefer something else. But she pushed her head back against the headrest, replaced the glasses and closed her eyes. Jed made a weary sound and stretched himself out on the backseat and Cameron headed west.

Grace slept. Not the kind of sleep she got in her bed. This was a deep calm. With the music playing and the soft hum of the motor she was unusually relaxed. Her typical day in a car was driving to and from the office in rush-hour traffic before fighting for a parking space.

She opened her eyes a few times over the following hour or so and watched as the landscape changed. The sugar cane farms were replaced by cattle and pasture and the homes became more infrequent the farther they drove. They didn't speak, which suited her fine and he seemed as content as she was to listen to the music and enjoy the scenery.

The smelly hound in the back didn't stir and she was grateful for that.

Cameron pulled into a roadhouse midmorning, where they refueled and grabbed coffee to go.

"Pat will want to feed us when we arrive," he told her as they walked back to the car. "But if you're hungry we can—"

"I'm fine," she said. "I had a big breakfast." She reached into her handbag and pulled out a small paper bag. "I have muffins for the road."

Cameron grabbed the bag and took a look inside. "You've been holding out on me for the past hour and a half?"

Grace colored. His words smacked of intimacy. And she wondered how she would hold out being with him for the next few days. Because it seemed so incredibly normal to be walking beside him in the morning sunshine.

She shrugged lightly. "I did some baking yesterday. Help yourself."

Cameron took a muffin and ate it in about three bites. "It's good." He unlocked the car and stared at her. He waited until she was in the car before getting in himself. He patted the dog and then wiped his hands on a towel on the backseat. "So, what else can you cook?"

"I just took a Thai cooking class. And I make some mean sushi."

He looked like she'd said rat bait. "Oh. Sushi…I've never tried it."

"It's delicious," she said and clicked her tongue.

His gaze went instantly to her mouth and Grace couldn't stop her lips from pouting ever so slightly. There was something intensely erotic about him looking at her mouth and she felt the sensation right down to the blood in her bones. He turned away before she did, but Grace swore she saw something in his eyes, a kind of raw hunger that turned his irises to a deep chocolate. He cleared his throat and started the engine and she tried not to think about how warm her skin was. Or how much she liked the sensation.

Burdon Creek *was* in the middle of nowhere. It was a quiet, sleepy-looking place that had aura of another time about it. They drove slowly down the one main street and continued past the gas station. The farm was about ten miles from the town center and when they arrived Cameron got out of the car to open the rickety gate.

The house stood at the end of the long gravel driveway. It was old, but she saw where the contractors had worked hard to repair the roof and the large veranda. It needed painting on the outside and the garden was overrun with twisted bougainvillea vine.

There were stables some way from the house and a large machinery shed. A boy in dark overalls was walking across the yard and came over to greet them. It was Dylan, and when they got out Cameron shook his hand.

"I've been feeding the horses," Dylan announced, looking immensely pleased with being in charge of the task.

"The neighbor supplied the kids with a couple of horses for the weekend," Cameron told her as he let the dog out. The big drooling beast made his way around the car and Grace held herself rigid as he pushed against her leg.

"He wants a pat," Dylan told her and came over and rubbed the dog's head. "He always wants pats. Nan said we could get a dog once we get a fence around the house."

"Cam!"

They all turned at the sound of the loud greeting. A sixty-something woman stood on the porch with a walking stick in her hand. She had a mop of frizzy gray hair and a beaming smile. Cameron walked across the yard and hugged the woman close when he reached her. Grace stood still, watching the exchange. She'd never been a hugging sort of person. Even with her family. Of course, it was impossible to avoid it with Evie and M.J., because they were both warm and affectionate, but her parents and Noah seemed to respect her need for personal space.

"Who's this?" the woman asked as both silvery brows rose. "A girl?"

Grace walked across and stood at the bottom of the short stairway. "I'm not really a girl...I'm the decorator."

Cameron laughed and once the introductions were made

Patricia Jennings invited them inside. The house was in various states of repair. Plasterers had been in to replace walls and most of it required painting. There was some furniture scattered throughout certain rooms and the kitchen had received a full renovation.

"Take a seat," Pat invited as they entered the kitchen. "I'll put the coffee on."

Grace sat down while Cameron headed back outside to retrieve their luggage. She placed her handbag on the chair beside her. "Where's Emily?" she asked.

"Putting the baby down for a nap," Pat said and smiled. "I have to say how committed she's become to her studies since you've been helping her. She really wants to finish high school, which isn't an easy task for a young mother. She has had a hard time of it since Riley came along." Pat raised her brows. "I thought of shifting her to a new school but she wanted to stay where she was."

"She's been bullied?"

"A little," Pat replied. "Teenage girls can be cruel."

Grace knew about that firsthand. Her first twelve months at boarding school had been fraught with teasing and isolation. "Are you looking forward to moving here permanently?" she asked, politely making conversation.

Pat turned around, swinging mugs in her hands. "Oh, yes. The kids will love being able to run around and Dylan becomes quite the man of the house when we're here, fixing things and doing chores." Her wrinkled face grew somber. "Maybe he's too grown-up sometimes. We used to be really close. But with the little ones needing me I just don't seem to have the time for him that I used to. I was so worried about Dylan at one stage—but then Cameron came along and he's a changed boy since he's had a man's influence in his life." Her pale blue eyes regarded Grace and she smiled. "Officer Jakowski was a godsend to us. You're a lucky woman."

Grace knew what she meant and quickly set her straight. "Oh, we're not... It's not like that. We're just..."

"Just what?" Pat asked as she poured coffee.

Grace briefly explained how their mothers had been inseparable since they were in their teens, and that Noah was his closest friend. "We've know one another a long time."

Pat nodded, like she suspected there was more to it than that. "It's good of you to come and help us this weekend," she said and brought the coffee to the table. "It's been hard trying to sort through everything, and with the two little ones still missing their daddy I've had my hands full."

Grace couldn't imagine how difficult it had been for the other woman. She looked weary and not in the best of health. But she obviously loved her grandchildren.

"The kids are lucky to have you."

Pat smiled warmly. "I'm the lucky one. When Lynnie..." She stopped for a moment and took a deep breath. "That's my daughter. When she went off the rails this last time I knew I had to do something for the children's sake. Dylan was at such an impressionable age and the younger children needed to be cared for. Their father was killed over a year ago."

"Cameron told me."

Pat tutted. "It was very sad. He's wasn't a bad sort of man. At one time I'd hoped he and Lynnie might have worked things out. But he wasn't prepared to live with an addict. Can't say I blame him." Pat grabbed milk from the refrigerator and placed it on the table. She sat down heavily in a chair and stared at Grace. "You're very beautiful. I can see why Cameron's interested in you."

Grace stopped herself from denying it and put a little sugar in her mug. "It's complicated."

"Life generally is," Pat said agreeably. "I was married for thirty-five years to a good man. When he passed away three years ago I lost the love of my life."

Grace felt a sudden stab of envy. She'd never experienced anything even remotely resembling that. And the look on Pat's face was the same look she saw on Evie's face, and Callie's and her mother's.

True love. When had she become so cynical about it? Her bland relationships with Dennis and Erik hadn't left her brokenhearted. There had been a definite lack of intimacy, both sexual and emotional. She'd lost her virginity to Dennis when she was twenty-two, five months after they'd begun dating. There were no fireworks in the bedroom, though. And in hindsight, very little chemistry between them. Erik had been more sophisticated and more sexually demanding, but that had only created a greater wall between them. Her continued lack of response to him between the sheets had finally made him walk out the door. In some ways she'd been relieved when it had ended.

She remembered the conversation she'd had with Cameron about marriage. It was easy to hide behind the idea that a woman couldn't have it all. And she had told herself she didn't want that time and time again. She had her career and her driving ambition. She wore shoes that probably cost more than the woman sitting opposite her spent on clothes in a year and never let anyone get too close. And that, she realized, was why she'd never felt truly whole. The emptiness had grown bigger as she gotten older, and each year she filled that space with more work, more ambition. She had a half-lived life. But the thought of anything else, anything…more…rattled her to the very foundation of her soul.

"You know, it's the little things that I miss most," Pat said with a soft sigh. "Like how he used to always make that first cup of tea in the morning. Or how he'd mow the lawn and then come inside smelling like cut grass. And we'd play cards every Sunday night." She looked across the table. "There's a lot to be said for the love of a good man."

Grace had no intention of responding to that. Fortunately Dylan and Cameron returned to the kitchen with their luggage and Pat suggested they settle into their rooms. She was surprised to find they weren't going to be in the main house, but in a separate cozy cottage about fifty meters from the mudroom and behind what looked like an old vegetable garden.

Two small children, a boy about four and a girl a couple years older, both with grubby faces and bare feet, raced around to greet them and Pat quickly introduced her other grandchildren, Thomas and Isabel.

"You'll be comfortable here," Pat assured her as they walked across the yard. "This was renovated first, and when we came for weekends we lived here until the house was ready. It used to be a workers' cottage many years ago, when the farm was a working cattle station and before the land was all subdivided."

Grace smiled, walked through the front door and was pleasantly surprised. Although sparsely furnished, it had lovely polished wood floors and high ceilings. It was clean and tidy and inviting.

"You'll have more privacy here than in the house with me and these adorable hellions," she said and gestured to the children zooming up and down the hall making airplane sounds with their arms outstretched.

Pat rounded up the kids and they all left once Grace's bags had been brought into the small hallway, and not before the older woman told them to come back to the main house for lunch in an hour. Once they were gone she turned to find Cameron standing behind her, one shoulder leaning casually against the doorjamb that led into the living room.

*So much for chaperones!*

"Okay?" he asked.

"It's nice," she replied as she peered into the bedroom off the hall. A large bed filled the room, covered in a crisp white

overlay. There was a neat vanity and narrow armoire. She
walked across the threshold and turned around. "I'm sure
I'll be quite comfortable."

Cameron moved forward and grabbed her bag. "You might
want to ditch the leather jacket and change," he suggested as
he dropped the luggage into her room. "We'll be painting a
little later."

She nodded and cleared her throat. "Um…where are you
sleeping?"

He pointed down the hall. "Miles away—so don't fret."

Grace flushed hotly. "I'm hardly fretting."

He smiled and her insides flipped over a little more than
usual. He looked good when he smiled, even more handsome.
And he had nice hair, she noticed, like the color of beechwood
honey. She remembered how it had felt caught between her
fingers and the memory made her hands tingle. The small-
ness of the room created a sudden intimacy and Grace sensed
a shift in the mood between them. She stepped back and col-
lided with the foot of the bed. "Well, I'll just get changed."

"Sure," he said and headed for the door, but suddenly he
stopped and turned. "What were you and Pat talking about
in the kitchen?"

*Love*…

"The kids," she replied, and placed her handbag on the
vanity. "And the house."

"Was she matchmaking?"

"I set her straight," she replied with a shrug. "I told her
exactly how we feel about each other."

He looked at her oddly. "I doubt that," he said and then
grabbed his bag and headed off down the hallway.

Grace took about twenty minutes to unpack and change
into a pair of gunmetal-gray cargo pants and a long-sleeved
navy T-shirt and bright red sneakers. She left her hair pulled

back in a low ponytail and took off her watch. The last thing she wanted was paint spattered on her Rolex.

When she was done, she took a tour of the small house. There was one bathroom, the kitchen and dining area and the living room. The furniture looked new and the country-cottage print on the sofa and curtains suited the place. There was also a small fireplace and a thick hearth rug in muted greens.

Emily arrived, books in hand, and announced she would be studying in the kitchen in the main house. They chatted for a couple of minutes before she left to start studying.

"Ready?"

Grace turned on her heels. Cameron stood in the doorway. He'd changed, too. He wore a pair of old jeans that had a hole in one knee and white T-shirt that was splattered in places with various shades of paint. Working clothes, she thought, and then felt ridiculously self-conscious in her immaculate two-hundred-dollar cargo pants.

She swallowed hard. "Sure. Let's go."

Once they were outside he suggested a tour of the farm before they headed to the house for lunch. Grace agreed and followed him toward the old stables. Jed rose from his spot on the porch and ambled behind them. The stables were big and old and smelled musty and she wrinkled her nose when they walked through the wide doorway. She picked up another scent immediately and recognized fresh baled hay. It had a sweetish smell and quickly knocked off the old-barn odor.

Through to the other side of the building was a large paddock. Grace spotted two horses happily munching grass. "It's a lovely spot," she said as she crossed her arms over a fence post.

He turned around and half trapped her against the fence. "Is breathing in this fresh air making you feel all country inside?"

Grace didn't move. To escape she would need to press past him. Maybe touch him. She prepped her sharp tongue. "I'm all city—you know that."

"And yet, you're here."

"I was forced into it."

His eyes darkened to the color of melted chocolate. "I'd never force you into anything."

He stepped back and didn't say another word as he began to walk back toward the house. She felt bad. Of course she knew he wouldn't force her to do anything she didn't want to do. That wasn't his way.

"Cameron?" He stopped walking and waited for her to catch up. "I didn't mean anything by that."

He nodded. "Forget it. We should get back."

Lunch was outrageously delicious and filled with more carbs than Grace usually consumed in a month. Fresh baked bread accompanied roast chicken and gravy and a creamy potato dish that was so scrumptious Grace had two helpings. The kids chatted throughout the meal and the littlest one got potato in his hair.

Grace wasn't sure what she felt sitting with the fractured, yet incredibly loving family. Cameron seemed to fit effortlessly within their little group. It made the world she lived in suddenly seem painfully superficial. On the surface she appeared to have it all—career, success, money.

And yet, for more than the first time lately, she wondered what the worth of it all was? At that moment, she couldn't see or feel anything other than a startling realness during the hour she shared with Pat Jennings and her grandchildren. And the man she'd tried desperately to keep out of her heart for so long, but knew she never had.

Or ever would.

## Chapter Six

As Cameron watched Grace his chest tightened. She was laughing at something one of the kids said and looked so incredibly lovely he could barely get air into his lungs. He'd never seen her so naturally unguarded. She was still as picture-perfect as always in her pressed trousers and starched T-shirt and there wasn't a hair out of place. But there was something in her expression he hadn't seen before. She smiled at him, as though she knew he was thinking about her. Did she know it? Was it obvious?

"We should get started on the painting," he said.

Grace nodded and stood. "I'll help clean up the dishes first."

"Nonsense," Pat replied. "Leave the dishes to me. I can manage that even with my bad leg. The painting is too much for these old bones. Off you go. I'll make sure the kids don't disturb you."

Cameron stood and left the room and felt Grace's pres-

ence in his wake. He headed for the living room and spotted
a pile of drop cloths by the entrance. The room was sparsely
furnished and had only a sofa and small coffee table.

"Where do you want me?" she asked.

Cameron turned around. Her words sounded provocative
and gave his insides a jolt. He grabbed a couple of the drop
cloths and held them out to her. "You can place these over
the furniture while I prepare the paint."

"Sure," she said as she took them. The painting gear was
on the veranda and he headed outside. He stayed for a while
to sort through colors and clear his head. When he returned
to the living room Grace was sitting on the edge of the sofa.
She stood and waited while he placed the paint and brushes
by the door.

"What color are we going for?" she asked as she examined
the paint lids for swatches.

"You choose," he replied and lifted off both lids.

She looked at the tins and gestured to the warm beige tint.
"That one. And I think we should consider a feature wall."
She pointed to the long wall opposite the doorway. "Something darker—maybe the rich toffee. If we add a slipcover
over the sofa in the same shade it will pick up the color."

He half smiled, intrigued by the interest she showed. "Anything else?"

She bit down on her lower lip for a moment. "Perhaps a
lamp—one of those tall ones for the corner. With a low-watt
bulb it will cast some nice shadows around the room. And a
plush rug for the spot in front of the fireplace. And maybe a
couple of pictures for the walls." She raised her brows with
a kind of keen excitement. "You know, Evie has some furniture pieces in a storage shed that she hasn't used for years.
I think she'd let them go if she knew they were going to a
good home."

Her sudden enthusiasm captivated him and Cameron took a deep breath. "I thought you said you couldn't decorate?"

She looked at him. "I said I'd hired a decorator."

"To do what?'

She smiled. "To do what I asked."

He'd never known a woman so determined to do things her own way. "You'll talk to Evie?"

"Yes. In the meantime let's get started."

Cameron started preparing the paint and Grace grabbed a brush. "Do want to cut in?" he asked as he poured a small amount of paint into a plastic container.

"Sure." She glanced up at the high ceilings. "I'll need a ladder."

That's not all she needed, he thought, looking at her designer clothing and spotless shoes. "There's one outside, I'll get it."

He took off down the hall, silently cursing the way his insides were jumping all over the place. Being near her was making him nuts. He'd be glad when the painting started so the fumes could drown out the scent of the flowery fragrance she wore, which hit him with the force of a jackhammer every time she moved.

He inhaled a long breath and headed for the cottage.

Grace poked the brush into the paint and examined the color. She'd started cutting in the edges around the doorjamb when Cameron returned. He held something out to her.

"Here," he said. "Wear this."

Grace put down her brush and took the garment. She held the soft chambray shirt in front of her and shook her head in protest. "I couldn't possibly—"

"Wear it," he insisted. "You don't want to ruin your clothes. It's an old shirt."

It was an old shirt. But it was incredibly soft between her

fingertips. She nodded and slipped her arms into the sleeves. It was far too big and she rolled the sleeves up to an accommodating length and did the buttons up, but it was surprisingly comfy.

"Thank you," she said and forced herself to not think about how intimate it seemed to be wearing a piece of his clothing.

Cameron grabbed the roller and paint can. "No problem."

She went to speak again but her mouth remained shut. He smiled slightly and awareness rushed across her skin in an all-consuming wave. The white T-shirt he wore did little to disguise his broad shoulders and muscular arms. And his jeans were so worn and faded they amplified the ranginess of his lean hips and long legs.

Grace struggled to drag her eyes away. Everything about him was wholly masculine and she realized at that moment how naively she'd been denying it to herself for so many years. She'd never been attracted to a man the intense way she was attracted to Cameron.

They worked through the afternoon and by four o'clock she was exhausted. Her palms were pink and puckered from the constant pressure of the brush and her neck ached. But despite her pains, Grace was determined to push past her fatigue. She wouldn't give in. Cameron of course, was like a machine. He worked through the break Pat insisted they have, and because she wasn't giving in to her exhaustion, forced Grace to do the same. She quickly took a couple of massive gulps of icy homemade lemonade Pat had brought in on a tray to avoid looking like she was taking a breather, and climbed back up the ladder.

They had music playing softly in the background and the ugliest dog in world was stretched out beside the sofa, snoring the afternoon away.

"We should finish up soon." He'd stopped painting and

came over to the corner where she was propped up on the ladder. He looked up at her and held out his hand. "Come down."

Grace reached out and grasped his hand. He wrapped his fingers around hers and she felt the contact down to her toes. She stepped down the ladder and when her feet touched the floor her legs were strangely unsteady. She placed the container and brush on top of the small ladder and kept her hand in his.

Cameron looked directly into her eyes. "You have paint on your face."

Any other time Grace would have been immediately self-conscious. She usually hated mess and being untidy. But she was reluctant to break the easy mood that had developed between them over the course of the afternoon. "I guess I should go and wash up," she said quietly.

He grazed his knuckles across her left cheek. "I guess you should. It's water-based paint so you don't need to scrub too hard."

"Okay—well, I'll get going and…" Her words trailed off and she moved to pull away. But he didn't release her. "You still have my hand."

He half smiled. "So I do."

"I'll need it back if I'm to get rid of this paint on my face."

He released her immediately. "I'll clean up the brushes and the rest of the gear."

Grace stepped away and pulled her arms around herself. "Okay." She looked around the room. "We did a good job today." She turned to the exposed fireplace and the lovely pale coffee-colored wall framing it. "And it feels good to *do* something good." She gave a humorless laugh. "But I guess you know that already. You've always been generous with yourself." When he didn't say anything she raised a brow. "That was a compliment, not a dig."

Cameron stared at her. "With our history sometimes it's hard to tell the difference."

He was right and Grace experienced something that felt a lot like shame work its way across her skin. "Looks like our truce is working."

"We've gotten off to a pretty good start. No fights, no insults, for at least..." He checked his watch. "Eight hours."

"I've never liked fighting with you," she admitted. "It was just easier than thinking about...about anything else."

"I know."

She didn't respond and left the room as quickly as she could, making for the kitchen. After spending a few minutes with Emily to see how the studying was going, Grace walked back to the cottage.

A shower topped her list of things to do. Grace collected fresh clothes and toiletries and headed for the bathroom. The claw-foot bathtub was the first thing she saw and she was immediately seduced by the idea of a long soak. She quickly popped in the plug and played around with the water temperature. Once the water flowed she added her favorite Dior scented bath foam and stripped off her clothes.

It took close to ten minutes to fill the tub, but finally she slipped into the bubbly water and stretched out her legs. Grace let out a heavy sigh and her body relaxed instantly. She'd had a long, exhausting day and was physically taxed, but had none of the mental fatigue she often experienced as a result of a fifteen-hour stretch in the office.

She rested her arms along the edge of the tub, closed her eyes and leaned her head back. A simple delight. But it felt better than anything had felt for a long time. When was the last time she'd spent the time to really relax? She couldn't remember. Since the accident she'd become even more wound up, more determined to be in control.

She took a deep breath and slipped a little farther down

into the water. A sound caught her attention but she kept her eyes shut. A creak followed, like a door opening. Had she not closed the door properly? *It's probably just the wind pushing the door open.*

Another creak followed. And another. It was the door. And it *was* opening.

Grace clamped her lids tighter. Surely Cameron wouldn't enter the bathroom? But when she finally found the courage to open her eyes, it wasn't Cameron standing by the bathtub.

It was Jed.

The smelly beast had pushed the door open far enough to invade her privacy and was sitting heavily on his haunches, drooling all over the floor. He made a sound, half growl, half whine.

"Shoo!" she demanded, looking around for her towel. It was on the sink where she'd left it. The smelly dog scooted closer and dropped his chin on the rim of the tub. "Go away."

He whined again and showed off his big teeth.

Grace pushed herself back as far as she could go. *I will not panic.* She heard footsteps in the house and quickly pulled herself together. Cameron was back.

*"Hot Tub!"* she yelled, knowing the nickname he hated would get his attention.

The footsteps grew louder and she heard a tap on the half-opened door. "Grace?"

"You're dog is drooling in my bathwater—get him out of here."

He laughed.

"It's not funny," she protested. "Please get him out of here so I can finish my bath."

Cameron laughed again. She was taking a bath? He hoped the rainwater tanks could support it. He called Jed to come out. The dog didn't come so he called him again. And again.

Damned dog.

"It's no use," she said shrilly. "He's got one paw up on the tub. If he gets in the water I swear I'll…I'll…"

He tried not to laugh and called the dog again. When Jed didn't respond he said, "So, can I come in?"

She was silent for a moment. "Well, yes…okay."

Cameron took a deep breath and pushed the door back. Sure enough, there was Jed, paw up on the rim of the tub, drool oozing from his mouth, and staring at Grace with what was clearly a serious case of puppy love. "He likes you."

Grace scowled at him and ducked down into the water. "Funny. Get him away from me."

"Come on, Jed," he said firmly. "Let's go."

He walked toward the bathtub and kept his gaze centered firmly on the dog.

*I will not look at her.*

But Jed had his own ideas and sprang up on his back legs, wagging his tail. Any second now, Cameron thought, and the dog would be in the water with Grace. He lunged for the animal and grabbed his collar. Grace screamed. Jed rose up on his back feet and splashed his front paws into the water. Grace moved against the back of the tub and the foamy water sloshed, exposing her creamy shoulders and the unmistakable swell of her breasts and his breath rushed out with a sharp kick.

*I am so not looking at her.*

But as the bubbles sloshed and rose her body was silhouetted against the opaque water. A body he'd touched that night on the beach. And suddenly looking at her was all he was good for. He glanced at her face and saw her green eyes shining with a kind of hot awareness.

Sex swirled around the steamy room—potent and powerful.

She used her hands to shield the parts she didn't want him seeing and that just kicked at his libido like an out-of-control sledgehammer. He could imagine sliding the soap across her skin, he could almost feel how smooth and slippery...

"Cameron...I...I..."

Grace's voice, barely a whisper, dragged him from his fantasies.

He pulled the dog back, grabbed his collar and with the animal firmly under control he spun him around and headed out of the room. Cameron shut the door and released Jed instantly. The dog scooted off, leaving a trail of wet paw prints in his wake.

Cameron let out a heavy breath, stood outside the bathroom door and rested his forehead against the jamb.

*Idiot...*

One glimpse of skin and he was done for. He wanted her so much.

And had two more weeks to do something about it.

Grace pulled herself out of the tub once the door clicked shut and hastily grabbed a towel. She rubbed herself dry and pulled on her clothes with less than her usual care.

*Cameron Jakowski saw me naked.*

Okay, not completely naked but close enough. Close enough that Grace knew that what she saw in his eyes was raw hunger.

She shoved her feet into flat sandals.

*No man has ever looked at me like that.*

His gaze had scorched her skin like a lover's touch. He'd looked like he wanted take her into his arms and kiss her passionately—right then, right there.

And the knowledge tapped into something inside her. Grace had never considered herself all that desirable. Erik's complaints about her lack of enthusiasm in the bedroom still echoed in her head. Dennis hadn't been as harsh, but she'd sensed his dissatisfaction with her, especially in the latter months they were together.

But those fleeting moments in the bathroom with Cameron made her feel so sexually charged that every part of her skin tingled. The truth pounded through her like the loud beat of a drum.

She wanted to make love with Cameron.

And she knew, without a doubt, that he wanted it, too.

What had happened between them at Evie's wedding should have knocked the truth into her. But she'd spent a week in a kind of hazy denial. And now, all of a sudden, she knew it, felt it, and could almost taste the reality of it. And it scared her. She feared losing control. Of being vulnerable. Because Cameron could do that to her. He'd always made her feel that way. He'd always had a secret, almost seductive power over her.

Grace checked her hair in the mirror and saw it was doing a faux impression of being straight as it fought for release from its ponytail. She tucked some stray pieces behind her ears and grabbed her toiletry bag before she headed from the room.

She dropped her things off in the bedroom and walked through the house. Jed was in the small living room, spread out in front of the fireplace, his deep snoring sounding as if he needed an inhaler. She grimaced at the sight of his pink-and-fleshy gums and then left him to his nap.

In the kitchen she noticed an aluminum tray on the countertop and immediately popped the lid, inhaling the scent of delicious-looking pasta. Obviously from Pat, Grace found the other woman's consideration heartwarming. The clock on the wall read a quarter past seven and her grumbling stomach figured it was soon time for dinner. She popped the tray in the oven and set it to a low heat.

"Hey."

She pivoted on one heel. "I see Pat prepared dinner for us," she said easily. "I've just starting reheating but it shouldn't take long. I thought I would—"

"Grace?"

She took a breath. He stood in the doorway, arms crossed, seeming like he had something to say but wasn't quite sure how to say it. Still wearing the paint-splattered T-shirt and ridiculously sexy jeans he looked so good her traitorous belly flipped over. "What?"

He shrugged. "About before…I want to apologize."

Grace fiddled with a tea towel to do something with her hands. "It was my fault. I should have made sure the door was shut properly."

"That's not what I meant."

Grace cursed the color she knew rose up over her collar. "Oh, well I—"

"Things have changed between us," he said, cutting her off. He ran a hand through his hair and she watched him without taking a breath. "For years we've been skirting around it, avoiding it, pretending that what happened between us when we were young didn't matter. But it does matter, Grace, and it's stopped us from being anything to each other, if that makes sense. We're not friends, we're not enemies…we're not lovers…we're just stuck somewhere in between."

"I can't—"

"I won't pretend I don't want you, Grace. Not anymore."

She stilled instantly. In another time, another life, she would have shot him down immediately. Because now, despite the voice in her head telling her that her life was about to get way more complicated, she wanted him, too.

Even though she knew it wouldn't be enough. She was going back to New York in two weeks. Starting something with Cameron would be madness. It might be mind-blowing. It might be exactly what she needed to help ease the dreadful grief and guilt that clung to her every pore.

But when she opened her mouth, prudence foolishly disappeared and something else altogether came out. "Is that why I'm here?" she asked. "Because you want to get me into bed?"

He took a moment to respond. "Not…entirely."

She couldn't help but smile. Another man might have denied it. But Cameron was too honest to play games. "If that's the case, then I guess we'll just see what happens."

His brows shot up. "And let nature take its course, you mean?"

She dropped the tea towel on the counter. "In a way. I don't see the point in either of us getting worked up over something that hasn't happened—or might never happen."

He stared at her. "So, it *is* mutual?"

She made a job of looking for plates and cutlery to avoid the question. When she'd unearthed both she turned back around and found Cameron still watching her. "Well," she said with a sigh, "I'm hardly the type of woman who lets just anyone put his…I mean…his hand…up my dress." The heat got her then, flaming her cheeks, and she gripped the plates until her fingers were white.

He didn't say anything for a moment. He looked at her though—that look she'd suddenly come to think of as the sexiest look in history. "Okay, Grace. We'll take things slowly, if that's what you want." He muttered something about taking a shower and turned on his heels, and Grace got back to her task before he'd even left the room.

Cameron took a cold shower and did his best to clear the chaos raging through his thoughts. Of course, it didn't work. And by the time he'd dressed, lingered in his room for what seemed like an eternity, and then finally headed back to the kitchen, Grace was still behind the counter, chopping and dicing vegetables for a salad.

He fed the dog and set the table, trying to ignore how absurdly domestic it seemed, moving around the kitchen together, not speaking, but feeling as though they had been doing it this way for years.

They ate dinner and even opened the bottle of wine Pat had left in the refrigerator. Once their plates were empty and the dishes cleared, they were left at the table, lingering over the remainder of their wine.

She looked different, he thought, then realized it was probably one of the few times he'd seen her without makeup. He liked it. She looked younger and less uptight. She smiled and it ignited something inside him. There'd been a kind of easy camaraderie between them over dinner and he didn't want that to change, but she looked so fetching with her clean face and bright smile, he could hardly think of anything other than hauling her into his arms and kissing her madly.

"You're great with the kids," she said and he got his mind back on track.

"Thank you," he said. "They're easy to like."

"You'll make a good dad."

Cameron's heart suddenly pounded behind his ribs. Could she know that's what he wanted? That he was aching for a family of his own? "One day, I hope so. You know, you're not bad with kids yourself."

She made a scoffing sound. "I'm a train wreck."

"Emily doesn't think so," he said quietly. "She told me you've been patient and understanding, but also firm when she loses concentration."

"Well, she's a good student, despite her lack of confidence. Did you know she wants to go to college?"

He nodded. "She's got ambition."

"Which isn't a bad thing."

"I didn't say it was."

She fingered the stem of her wineglass. "No, you didn't. But…"

"But what?" he prompted.

"You didn't always feel that way."

He pushed back in his chair. "You mean about *your* ambition? I was young and had ideas about the kind of future I wanted. Just like you did, Grace. Only mine were small-town and yours were big-city."

She looked at him. "You were angry."

"I was dumped," he said bluntly. "What did you expect? Roses and violins?"

"I guess not. I didn't deliberately set out to…to hurt you." She drew in a tight breath. "In hindsight I shouldn't have started anything knowing how I felt about wanting a career. But I was young and starry-eyed. Even career girls get swept away sometimes."

His heart pumped. "By what?"

Her shoulders rose fractionally. "By romance, I guess. By that first kiss when I was sixteen. By the way you didn't rush me to sleep with you, even though we were dating for a few months."

"I thought we had…" He stopped, remembering how much he'd wanted her back then. "Time."

She looked into her glass for a moment, and then glanced upward. "Well, for what it's worth—I'm sorry for the way I behaved back then. These past couple of months I've had a lot of time to think. It sounds cliché, but there's something life-altering about facing your own mortality. When the car crashed I had about thirty seconds to consider all the mistakes I've made, all the people I've hurt in one way or another. It was a sobering half minute."

"Apology accepted."

She offered a bittersweet smile and stood, scraping the chair back. "We did have a nice three months, though. Life was way less complicated then. Do you think anyone ever suspected?"

Cameron stood and moved around the small table and took hold of her hands. "My mother figured it out. I'm not sure about anyone else. Noah's never said anything to me."

"I told Evie a long time ago," she confessed. "Did you know you were my first kiss?"

He rubbed her hands with his thumbs. "I kinda guessed."

"Was I that bad?"

"Not at all," he said gently. "But you seemed a little surprised."

"I was," she admitted. "At school I was into books and not boys. It didn't exactly make me Miss Popularity. And you'd never shown any interest...I mean, before that night of my birthday."

He chuckled. "Oh, I was interested. But you were too young and my best friend's sister."

"So what changed that night?"

"Seeing you standing in the doorway," he said and reached up to twirl a lock of her hair. "When I arrived everyone else was by the pool, but you were inside, and alone. You looked beautiful in that little blue dress. Before that I just..." He shrugged and smiled. "I just wanted you to grow up quick so I could kiss you like I'd imagined doing so many times."

He bent his head and kissed her softly. It wasn't like the night on the beach. This kiss was gentler, sweeter somehow. He wasn't sure how long they stood like that—just kissing, just holding the back of her neck tenderly with his one hand while the other lay against her hip. Grace gripped his arms and held on, and he enjoyed the feel of her mouth against his own and the soft slide of her tongue.

When the kiss ended Cameron laid his forehead against her. "Well," he whispered hoarsely. "That seems pretty natural to me. Good night, Grace," he said softly and released her. "Go and get some sleep. I'll lock up."

She rocked on her heels. He knew sleep wasn't what either of them wanted. But he was offering her an out and he knew she'd take it.

She said good-night and walked from the room without saying another word.

## Chapter Seven

Cameron didn't sleep more than two hours. With Grace only meters away down the hall he lay awake most of the night and stared at the ceiling. When he'd finally had enough of fighting the sheets he swung out of bed and got dressed. It was just after seven and he could hear Dylan in the yard with his little sister. Cameron looked out of the window and spotted Isabel racing around her brother as he snuck out from the chicken pen clutching a basket in his hands. His sister gave him no peace as he crossed to the house and it made Cameron smile. Lauren had been like that, he remembered fondly. Six years younger, his sister had hung from his every word when they were growing up.

He was still smiling as he left the room, then headed for the kitchen once he'd let Jed outside. Cameron made coffee, drank a cup and was just rinsing off the utensils when he heard a curse. A very loud curse. He stood still and waited. Then it came again.

Grace's voice was unmistakable. But the words coming out of her mouth were unlike any he'd heard from her before. He took off past the living room and headed for the hall. The profanity started again and he stalled outside her bedroom.

"Grace," he said quietly as he tapped on the door. "Are you all right?"

Nothing for a moment, then a clipped, "Yes…fine."

"You sound like you're in—"

"I'm fine, like I said," she insisted. "I'm just having a little trouble with my… I forgot to bring something to this forsaken place, that's all. Can you please leave me alone?"

"Sure," he said, grinning to himself. "I've made coffee."

"Whatever," she mumbled and he heard the frustrated banging from behind the shut door.

Something was up, but he didn't press the issue. He walked back to the kitchen and opened the refrigerator, mulling over the contents. When nothing took his fancy he shut the door and reached for a glass, and then stopped dead in his tracks. Grace stood in the doorway.

And she looked thunderous. "Don't say a word," she warned.

Cameron bit back the urge to smile. "About what?" he asked innocently.

Both her hands snapped up to frame her head. "About this!"

Now he smiled, because he couldn't help himself. Her hair, usually so straight and severe, bounced around her face in a mass of wild curls. Untamed and out of control, she'd never seemed more beautiful in her life. "It looks—"

"I forgot my straightener," she said with a sniff.

"What?"

"Hair straightener," she replied. "My flatiron. And now I have to deal with this *mess*."

He laughed then and she didn't like that one bit. "Your hair looks fine," he assured her. "It looks pretty."

She plucked at a few strands. "It's not pretty. It's not fine," she retorted, then let out a long breath. "You think I'm over-reacting?"

Cameron raised a hand. "Don't accuse me of thinking."

That made her laugh and she clutched her fingers together. "No one has seen me like this since...well, I can't remember the last time."

"You look good," he said and passed her a cup. "Drink up. We've got work to do."

She took the coffee and patted her stomach. He noticed she was wearing his shirt again. He liked that. "I'm hungry. Feed me first."

Cameron's libido did a leap. The mood between them seemed oddly playful and it made him think about fisting a handful of that glorious hair and kissing her neck. "I make a mean batch of scrambled eggs," he said and begrudgingly pushed back the idea of kissing her. "Feel like risking it?"

She nodded, perched on a bar stool and sipped her coffee. "I'm game."

He got what he needed from the refrigerator and began cooking while Grace quietly drank her coffee and stared at the linoleum countertop. She looked like she had something on her mind and he wondered if she'd spent the night staring at the ceiling like he had. After a while she put the cup down and linked her hands together.

"Why did you kiss me last night?"

Cameron stopped whisking eggs and stared at her. His chest tightened. "Because I wanted to. Because you're beautiful." He smiled. "The usual reasons."

"You know I'm leaving in two weeks?"

"Yes."

"And you know I'd never move back?"

Cameron put the eggs aside. "You wouldn't?"

Grace shrugged. "I don't belong in this world, Cameron. I don't belong in *your* world."

"Is that your way of letting me down gently?" he asked, and noticed her green eyes were suddenly luminous as she looked at him. "Even though you're not denying there's an attraction here?"

"But when a relationship is only based on strong physical—"

"Were you in love with the suit?" he asked quickly. "Or the doctor?"

"No."

"Have you ever had an intimate relationship just for the sheer fun of it?"

Her gaze narrowed. "I don't believe in casual sex."

"I'm not talking about something casual, Grace. I'm talking about having a relationship without laying down a whole lot of ground rules."

"I don't do that," she said hotly.

Cameron's brows shot up. "You don't?"

"Okay, maybe I do," she replied. "I like to be in—"

"In control," he said, cutting her off. "Yeah, I get that about you, Grace. But sex shouldn't be about control. It should be fun."

She glared at him. "Just because I take things seriously, that doesn't make me an uptight prig. I know how to have fun. Maybe my relationships with Dennis and Erik weren't all fireworks and passion. And maybe I did insist on separate apartments and avoided having them stay over because I'm too independent about have to be in control of *everything*. Maybe I'm all that and more…but it doesn't mean I'm sex-starved or frustrated or that I'm going to jump into the nearest bed I can find."

*If I had any sense I'd forget all about her.*

But he was all out of sense when it came to Grace.

"I wasn't suggesting you should," he said and bit back a grin. "Just, to not dismiss the idea entirely."

She shrugged. "I'm not good at relationships. I'm not good with people. With men. I always seem to make them leave." Her hands came to her chest and she held them there. "Do you know that I've only ever trusted three men in my whole life," she said softly and with such rawness his insides constricted. "My father, my brother…" She let out a long sigh. "And you. I know it probably hasn't seemed that way."

"No," he said. "But things often aren't what they seem."

"Like what?" she asked.

"Like the way I've always felt about you, Grace."

The words hung in the room. She didn't say anything else as they sat down for breakfast. They ate the eggs in a kind of forced silence. Grace offered to wash up and he didn't argue as he headed off. He'd said too much. Admitted too much. Her silence was like a swift slap in the face. It was a rejection. Again.

He was accustomed to it.

*Don't you ever learn, Jakowski?*

He left the room, mumbling something about paintbrushes and getting started on the painting.

By eight-thirty Grace headed for the main house. Pat was in the kitchen and greeted her with a broad smile.

"The kids are in the stable," the older woman explained. "Waiting for kittens to be born. A stray arrived last time we were here and I didn't have the heart to call animal welfare." She looked at Grace. "Did you sleep okay?"

Grace patted down her curls. "Yes, thank you. The cottage is very comfortable."

"But small," Pat said, grinning. "Too small and snug for

one old lady, four kids and a baby. But for you and Cameron—
I imagine snug would be good."

Grace's cheeks flamed. "Like I said, we're not—"

"I know what you said," Pat said cheerfully and plopped a
tea bag into a cup. "But I also know what I see. Even the brav-
est man might be afraid of letting his true feelings show," Pat
said quietly. "If he believes he's going to get hurt."

*Like the way I've always felt about you…*

That was just it. He had let his feelings show.

And it terrified her. For years she'd handled his antagonism
and sarcasm—that was easy. That she could combat with insults of her own. This was something else. Knowing he had
feelings for her, still had feelings for her, made it impossible
to keep denying her own feelings…the ones that were madly
beating around in her heart.

The back door opened and Dylan entered excitedly. Cameron soon followed. He glanced at Grace and then turned to
Pat. "Looks like rain in the distance."

"Rain?" Pat's expression widened. "Wouldn't that be
lovely? We need a downpour to fill up the rainwater tanks.
What I'd give for something more than the two-minute shower
I have every time we're here."

Grace looked at Cameron, instantly mortified when she
remembered the luxurious soak in the tub she'd had the afternoon before. She hadn't considered water preservation.
She'd only given a thought to herself. His eyes were dark as he
watched her, as if he knew her thoughts. Shame raced across
her skin. What hadn't he said something to her?

"I'll have one-minute showers from now on," Grace told
Pat. "You can use my saved minute for your bathtub."

Pat grinned broadly. "You're a sweet girl, Grace." Her
crinkled eyes zoomed in on Cameron. "You shouldn't let this
one go in a hurry."

Cameron smiled and leaned against the doorjamb. "I'll see what I can do."

It was a highly inflammatory thing to say and Grace's skin warmed immediately. "We should get started on the painting," she said and avoided the curious look on the older woman's face as she took a step. "I'd like to work with Emily this afternoon."

"The main bedroom needs doing," he said. "We can start there."

She didn't say another word and swiveled on her heels. In the main bedroom seconds later, she saw that Cameron had already moved the furniture to the center of the room and covered it with a drop cloth.

"Grace?"

He was behind her and she turned immediately. "What color today?" she asked, ignoring the thunderous beat of her heart behind her ribs. "Perhaps a pale—"

"Grace," he said again and with more emphasis. "We've got another two days here—so let's not get hung up on what I said earlier, okay?"

She shrugged. "It's forgotten already." She picked up a can of paint and thrust it toward him. "Let's start."

He took the paint and grabbed her hand before she could escape. "There's no need for you to be afraid of me."

"I'm not," she refuted.

"You're shaking."

Was she? Grace looked at her hands. The quiver was undeniable. "Let me go."

"Not until you tell me what's wrong."

"I can't," she said and tried to pull away. "I can't talk to you."

"Grace?"

It was too much. Too much honesty. Too many feelings were emerging and she had no idea how to handle it...or to handle him. She shouldn't have said anything. She should have worked on getting through the next two days without getting involved. But she lay awake for half the night, thinking about him…thinking about his kiss, his touch, and how suddenly it was the one thing she wanted more than anything else.

And it couldn't be.

She wasn't cut out for a relationship with him. She was going home in two weeks. Back to New York and everything familiar.

Grace took the brush and headed for a corner. She turned around and faced him, her back to the wall. "I just want to get through the weekend."

"Is being with me such a hardship?" he asked quietly.

"No," she admitted and looked sideways. "Which is exactly my point." Grace twirled the brush between her fingers. "I'm not going to sleep with you."

He looked tempted to smile. "I don't remember asking you to."

She plucked at the sleeve of the shirt that had become incredibly comfortable against her skin. She had the silly thought she might just keep it after the weekend was over.

"But you said…"

"I said what?" he queried. "That I want you?"

She exhaled. "Yes."

"So, I want you. It doesn't have to mean the end of the world, Grace," he said quietly. "It doesn't have to mean anything."

"Good," she said and pushed back her shoulders. "Because it doesn't." Grace turned on her heels, determined to ignore him and pretended to focus on painting.

Three hours later, and without more than half a dozen words said between them, the room was finished. Lunchtime loomed and Pat stuck her head in the doorway just as Cameron was pulling drop cloths off the bed, and told them to come to the kitchen. Grace ducked past the older woman, muttering something about washing up first and he didn't stop her.

He headed off to do the same once the bedroom was back in order. But he didn't find Grace in the cottage. She was outside with Isabel, examining a low branch on a citrus tree, which was weighed down by its fruit. He stood by the cottage steps and watched the exchange. With her hair down, her jeans spattered with paint and his old shirt hanging loosely off her shoulders she looked so incredibly lovely his chest felt like it would implode. Only Grace could do that to him. Only ever Grace.

Isabel laughed at something Grace said and she pulled a piece of fruit off the tree.

*She really is good with kids.*

But she didn't want them. That should have sent him running. Because he wanted children. The damnable thing was, he wanted to have them with Grace.

It took ten minutes to clean up, switch T-shirts and head back to the main house. He'd heard Grace come inside and head for the bathroom and left her to wash up as he made his way back to the main house. When he walked into the kitchen he quickly picked up that something was wrong. Pat and Dylan stood opposite one another and both faces were marred with a stricken look.

"What's up?" he asked as the back screen door banged behind him.

"It's Thomas," Pat said quickly, looking ashen. "He's gone missing."

Cameron stepped forward. "Missing? How long ago?"

Dylan shrugged his bony shoulders. "I'm not sure. Could be an hour or more. I thought he was with Isabel in the stable."

"Isabel was the last person to see him?" Cameron asked. Another shrug. "Dunno."

"Let's ask her, okay?"

Pat called the girl to come into the kitchen. Isabel couldn't remember when she'd last seen her brother and Cameron's instincts surged into overdrive. "We'll look around the house first," he assured Pat. "In all his favorite spots."

Grace entered the room and he told her what was happening.

"I'll help you look," she said and headed directly back out through the mudroom.

Fifteen minutes later, after every possible hiding place had been exhausted around the perimeter of the house, and they called his name repeatedly, Cameron knew they needed to widen the search.

"You head next door," he told Dylan. It was about one mile to the nearest neighbor and Cameron knew the boy would cover the ground quickly. "Grace and I will cut across the back paddock and head east. He can't have gotten too far. You stay here with the girls," he said to a worried Pat. "And call me if he comes back. Also, call the local police station and alert them to what's going on—tell them we're coordinating a search and you'll get back to them within the hour if we need help."

While he gave Dylan instructions he noticed Grace packing a small bag with water and cereal bars she'd found in the pantry. Within minutes they were outside and winding their way past the stables and through the barbed-wire fence.

"Any idea where he might be?" she asked as he held the wire apart while she slipped through.

They both stood and stared at the endless miles of pasture ahead of them. "Just a hunch he'd head this way. He knows not to go near the road because Pat has drummed road safety awareness into all the kids. This way seems logical."

She nodded. "Could he get far ahead of us?"

"Possibly. If he's just walking and not distracted." He raised his hand in an arc. "We'll keep about thirty meters apart. And watch for holes in the ground. I don't want you breaking any bones."

She nodded and walked off, creating space between them. And then they started walking, tracking across the undulating ground, looking for signs, anything that might indicate a little boy had come wandering this way. They were about ten minutes into it when his phone rang. When he finished talking and slipped the phone back into his pocket he noticed Grace had moved toward him a little.

"Who was that?" she asked in a loud voice.

"Fish," he replied.

She frowned. "What does that mean?"

"It was Pat," he explained. "Apparently Isabel remembered Thomas saying he was going to find a fish for the cat. Cats like fish, right?"

"I'm not sure I'm following you."

Cameron pointed toward the horizon. "There are three water holes on this property."

She flipped her sunglasses off her nose. "Do you think he might have—"

"I'm not sure," he said quickly and started walking again. He could see Grace's concern in the narrowing of her features. "Don't worry—he'll be fine."

She nodded. "Okay. Let's pick up the pace."

They did so quickly and thirty minutes later came across a small dam. Cameron checked for footprints and found only those belonging to cattle and the tracks of a lone wallaby.

"Nothing here," he said and trudged back up the side and onto the flat.

"That's a good thing, right?" Grace asked and passed him a bottle of water from the small backpack she'd brought with her. "If he's not here he might be on his way back. Maybe he's home already?"

Cameron forced a smile at her optimism and took the water. "Maybe. Let's keep going, though. The closest neighbor in this direction is about another three kilometers from here."

Five minutes later he heard from Pat again. He told her to call the neighbors and say they were on their way and to contact the police again and keep them updated. His phone crackled and faded as he rang off.

"Reception's gone for the moment," he said to Grace as they headed off again. "From now on we just keep walking and looking."

She nodded and turned away. But not before Cameron saw the fear in her expression. He felt it, too, although he wasn't about to admit that to Grace. They continued their trudge across the undulating landscape and didn't speak, but the tension between them was unmistakable. A shared tension brought on by the building threat that they wouldn't find Thomas—that he was lost, injured or worse.

Cameron spotted the familiar rise of another water hole ahead. A few cattle bellowed in the distance and he saw Grace hesitate on her feet as she walked. He doubted she'd ever been anywhere near a cow. He picked up speed and called the little boy's name. Grace quickly did the same and within seconds they were both jogging. She was faster than he'd imagined, even over the rough terrain. He stayed pace with her and somehow they ended up side by side, moving swiftly across the grass, avoiding stones and dips in the ground. He grabbed her hand and her tight grip seemed to push them harder and faster. Finally they reached the water hole and took long and hard steps up the embankment, sinking slightly in the unsteady clay underfoot.

"Cameron!"

Grace's voice echoed across the water as they both crested the rise. He saw Thomas immediately, on his belly, facedown in the murky water. He was at the water's edge in four strides and pulled the sodden, unconscious little boy into his arms, praying that they'd reached him in time.

## *Chapter Eight*

Grace heard a scream and realized it was her own terrified voice. Cameron trudged up the embankment with Thomas in his arms as she dropped the backpack.

Panic coursed through her blood. She'd felt that panic before. The accident and Richard's death came rushing back into her thoughts. She tried to shake off the memory, tried to act normally, tried to stop her knees from failing.

*Take a breath...one...two...*

Slow breathing helped whenever she experienced that rush of adrenaline, that same dreaded coldness whispering across her skin. Usually it happened when she was alone at night, or about to drift off to sleep...then the darkness wrapped her up and for a while she was back, trapped in that car, praying... hoping that someone would find her.

"Grace?"

Cameron's voice jerked her back into the present and she quickly pulled herself together as he laid the child on the ground. Thomas looked ghostly pale and she dropped to her knees beside him.

Her voice cracked when she spoke. "Is he breathing?"

Cameron shook his head and rolled the child over to clear water from his airway.

"Try my phone again," he barked and pulled the phone from his pocket as he turned Thomas onto his back again. "The nearest hospital is half an hour away so get an ambulance to meet us at the farm."

Grace grabbed the phone and hit the emergency number. Thankfully, there was a signal and she quickly made the call, ensuring an ambulance was on its way to the house. Time stretched like elastic, and what was seconds seemed like an eternity. She watched, horrified and fascinated as Cameron performed CPR and encouraged the child to breathe in between puffs of lifesaving oxygen. Finally Thomas spluttered and drew in a long gasp of air. She touched the boy's muddy hair soothingly as his breathing steadied. He opened his eyes and croaked out a word she couldn't understand. With instincts she hadn't known she possessed, Grace comforted Thomas and told him it would be all right. Cameron rocked back on his heels and closed his eyes and Grace touched his arm.

"You did it," she said, squeezing a little. "He's okay."

Cameron nodded and let out a long breath. "Let's get him home."

She nodded. "He's cold," she said, touching his pale face. Grace pulled a sweater from the small backpack and quickly threaded Thomas's arms into the sleeves and then took off her own jacket and tucked it around his small body. She rubbed his hands together for moment then looked toward Cameron. "Let's go."

She watched as he lifted the child effortlessly and held him against his chest. He walked back to the house as quickly as possible, and too emotional to speak, Grace followed. Pat and the rest of the children were waiting by the fence when they arrived and she heard Cameron's palpable sigh of relief at the sight of the ambulance in the driveway. Two medics were instantly on hand and rushed forward to take Thomas from Cameron's arms. Within minutes the little boy was wrapped in a thermal blanket and received the necessary attention from the officers.

Pat came to Grace's side, tears in her pale eyes. Without thinking, Grace braced one arm around the older woman's shoulder and held her tightly. Cameron spoke with the officers as they loaded Thomas into the vehicle.

"You should accompany him," Grace said to Pat. "Cameron will go with you. I'll stay here with Emily and the kids."

Pat nodded as tears welled and fell. "Thank you."

Minutes later Grace watched the ambulance skim down the gravel road following closely by Cameron's sedan. She hadn't said anything to him as he'd left. She hadn't needed to. The realization they could communicate with simply a look filled her blood, her skin, her very core.

She gathered the children and headed back to the house. Dylan seemed unusually quiet and she ushered him into the kitchen with the girls and Jed at their heels and made a quick meal of ham-and-cheese sandwiches. After they'd eaten Isabel raced off to her bedroom, too young to fully comprehend what had happened to their brother, while Emily went to bathe Riley and put him to bed. Dylan however, lingered by the sink. Aware that the boy was grappling with his emotions, Grace suggested a makeshift game of cards to help distract him until he chose to talk about how he was feeling.

It took about thirty minutes.

"Do you think he'll be okay?"

Grace dropped a card onto the table and chose another. "Of course he will."

"I should have watched out for him." He looked down-ward. "I wasn't watching. I wanted to muck around with the horses. I didn't want to get stuck watching the kids again. I forgot about him. I forgot and he disappeared. If Nan finds out she'll be really angry."

She heard the panic and pain in Dylan's voice and felt the need to comfort him. "I dropped my little sister on her head once," she admitted and looked at him over her cards. "I was supposed to be looking after her while my mother was out-side. We were twirling...but I got dizzy and dropped her."

"You *dropped* your sister?"

"Mmm-hmm."

Dylan's eyes widened. "Did you get into trouble?"

"Big-time," she replied. "For about ten seconds—until my mother realized how upset I was. She knew I didn't mean it. Just like your grandmother will know you didn't mean to for-get you were supposed to watch Thomas. It just happened."

He looked instantly relieved. "Do you think so?"

"For sure."

Dylan managed a little smile. "Thanks, Grace—you're the best."

A strange tightness constricted through the middle of her chest and she took a deep breath. When she heard a move-ment from the doorway she snapped her neck around. Cam-eron stood at the threshold.

"You're back?"

"Not for long," he said and came into the room. "Pat wants the kids to go to the hospital."

The blood leached from her face. "Is Thomas—"

"He's fine," Cameron assured her, and Dylan, who had jumped up in his chair. "No permanent damage. He's awake and he wants to see Dylan and the girls. I said I'd drive them back into town and they'll stay overnight at a motel. I'll pick them up tomorrow."

"I should get some things together for Isabel and tell Emily," she said as she stood and pushed the chair out. "She'll need to get Riley's booster seat for your car."

"That would be great. Come on, Dylan, let's get you ready." He went to turn, but then halted. "I should be back in a couple of hours."

Grace watched as Dylan scooted from the room and followed Cameron up the hallway. She gathered some fresh clothes for Isabel and then helped her change into jeans and a long-sleeved T-shirt.

Emily took some time gathering Riley's things together and Grace helped pack his baby bag.

"I feel bad," Emily said as she pulled on her jacket. "I've been wrapped up in taking care of Riley and studying. I haven't spent much time hanging out with the rest of the kids."

Grace patted the teenager's arm. "You can only do what you can," she said and picked up the bags. "Come on, your grandmother is waiting for you."

She stayed by the front steps as Cameron organized everyone into his car and packed their small bags into the trunk. He waved goodbye and drove off.

*And now I'm alone.*

Well, not exactly. Jed had ambled from his spot on the veranda and followed her back inside. Strangely, she didn't mind the company and allowed him to sit by her feet when she returned to the kitchen table. She shuffled the deck of cards and busied herself for a while with a game of solitaire. Once she was done Grace closed up the house and headed back to the cottage. She took a shower and the hot spray eased some of the tension tightening her shoulders. Now conscious of water shortages, she lingered for mere minutes, then changed into sweats and sat on the sofa in front of the television.

And quickly, like a runaway train, it hit her.

*Thomas could have died.*

For those few terrifying minutes she'd thought he wouldn't make it.

Fear closed her throat over and Grace sucked in some much needed air. She clutched her arms over her chest. Her lids dropped heavily as a familiar chill rushed over her skin. *I'm so cold.* She remembered that feeling. She remembered the fear and the helplessness. She remembered thinking she was going to die. And she remembered Richard's lifeless body, twisted and battered, beside her.

Jed groaned. She glanced at the dog. He pulled himself up, suddenly on alert. Grace quelled the unease narrowing through her blood. She heard a car door shut. Cameron. She got to her feet and rushed to greet him by the front door.

"He's fine," Cameron said as he walked across the threshold.

Grace clutched his arm. "Thank goodness."

"I need to feed the horses and then I'll hit the shower," he said and ran a weary hand through his hair. "Give me half an hour."

Grace released him and watched from the doorway as he walked back outside. The dwindling sun was all but gone when he returned to the cottage and headed for the bathroom. She fed the dog in the small mudroom and remained in the kitchen. Dinner would be pretty hit-or-miss, she realized when she opened the refrigerator. She pulled a couple of cans of soup from the cupboard and popped the contents into a saucepan to heat. Cameron came into the kitchen just as she had finished toasting thick slices of sourdough bread.

"You've been busy," he said as he passed the counter and saw the bread and green salad she'd prepared.

"It's not much," she said, feeling faintly embarrassed.

In low-slung faded jeans, white T-shirt and bare feet, he looked sexy and tempting.

Grace's skin warmed thinking about it and she turned back to her task.

"Do you need some help?" he asked and braced his hands on the edge of the counter.

She glanced sideways and avoided thinking about how his biceps flexed. "I'm good. So you said Thomas was doing well?"

"They want to keep him in for a couple of nights to be sure. But he's awake and talking."

She stopped what she was doing and looked at him. "Thanks to you."

"I wasn't alone," he said and stole a cucumber slice from the salad bowl.

"I didn't do much."

He leaned forward and crossed his arms. "You were there, Grace. You helped me do what needed to be done. You kept him warm," he reminded her. "And you comforted Dylan."

Her eyes widened. "You heard that?"

"About how you dropped Mary-Jayne on the head?" He grinned. "I heard. Explains a lot."

Grace laughed for probably the first time that day. And it felt good. "Poor M.J.," she said and returned to stirring the soup. "I love her dearly, you know."

"I think you have a great capacity for love, Grace," he said quietly. "You just don't show it."

The spoon rattled in the saucepan and she turned fractionally, avoiding his brown eyes. "Too hard."

"To admit you're human?"

She felt his questioning stare in the small confines of the kitchen. "Human? Am I? I've been called a lot of things."

"By me?" he prompted gently. "I guess that's true. We've said a lot of things to one another over the years."

"I deserved it," she said and stirred the soup some more.

"It's not like it isn't the truth. I know what I am. I know what people think of me."

"And what's that?"

"Oh, you know—that I'm a workaholic ice princess. Everyone has their place in a family, I guess. In mine, M.J. is the lovable one," she said. "Evie's the sensible one. And I'm the…smart one."

"And beautiful."

She shrugged and continued to stir.

"And talented in the kitchen. And good with kids." He looked at Jed lolling by the back door. "And dogs."

"Shocked even myself with that one," she said and spooned soup into two bowls. "Who would have thought?"

He grabbed the bread and salad, followed her to the table and sat down.

"I'm not fooled, Grace."

Grace slipped into a chair and looked at him. Really looked. Her heart—the same heart she'd tried hard to wrap in ice for so many years was suddenly pounding behind her ribs—and she was melting. The power he had over her—the power she'd denied because she was terrified of being vulnerable to him, of giving herself, of losing herself…suddenly that power made her want him even more.

She sighed out a breath. "Today I…I thought Thomas was going to die."

"Me, too."

"If he had…" The words caught, lingered, and then disappeared.

"But he didn't. He's safe. And so are you."

She looked up, emotion clogging her throat. Had she truly felt safe since the accident? Almost losing Thomas had brought all those memories back to the surface. And yet, being in the kitchen with Cameron, she somehow didn't have the usual emptiness in her heart.

"I feel safe now."

Cameron stilled. There was something incredibly vulnerable about Grace in that moment. He wanted to race around the counter and haul her into his arms. But resistance lingered. He couldn't be sure what she was feeling. And the idea of rejection suddenly waved like a red flag in front of him.

"I'm glad you feel safe with me."

She shrugged lightly. They ate in silence, but the tension in the room was extreme. Once the food was consumed and the plates taken care of, Cameron made his way to the sofa in the living room. She followed and stood by the fireplace.

"Are you joining me?" he asked and sat down.

She hesitated. The modest lamp in the corner gave enough light to see the wariness in her expression. "I should…go."

"Go where? To bed?" He checked his watch. "A little early for that, don't you think?"

A sigh escaped her lips and he watched her perfectly bowed mouth for a moment. Like everything about her face it was a thing of pure beauty. "I just thought—"

"Safe with me one minute, afraid of me the next. What's really going on with you, Grace?"

"I'm not afraid of you," she replied.

"Then sit down."

She took a few steps and dropped onto the sofa. "Okay, I'm sitting."

"Good," he said. "Now, talk."

She shook her head. "There's nothing to—"

"There is," he said, cutting her off. "I can see it in your eyes."

"Maybe I'm just upset over what happened today. I'm not made of stone, you know. If that little boy had—"

"But he didn't," Cameron said. "And we've already established that you're safe and sound here. So, talk to me," he insisted and rested an arm on the back of the sofa.

"What about?"

"Whatever's on your mind."

"Nothing is," she said and twisted her hands together.

Cameron pushed some more. "You could tell me about the crash and what happened that day."

Her breath caught. "I don't want to talk about it."

"Maybe you don't want to. But I think you need to."

"I have a shrink for that," she said and crossed her arms. "I went to counseling. I talked about *it* in exhausting detail and six sessions later I'm…I'm here."

"Here?"

"Home," she said quickly. "Crystal Point."

"I've never heard you call Crystal Point home before."

She shrugged. "My therapist thought being here would be good for me. I've told you all this already."

There was so much bite in her words Cameron knew she was holding back. "But you didn't say why?"

"I was in a car wreck."

"And your friend died?"

"Richard was a colleague," she said in a whisper. "And again, I've told you what happened. We were driving out to meet with a client and the car ran off the road. Richard died and I survived."

Cameron considered her words. "What happened then?" he asked and shifted to face her.

Her green eyes glittered. "We crashed and were trapped inside. That's the whole story."

Cameron wasn't convinced. "And how long were you trapped inside?"

She looked at him and shook her head. Shutters came up and a second later she stood.

"Grace?"

She shook her head again and headed for the fireplace. Cameron watched, mesmerized and confused, and he quickly pulled together his thoughts. Silence stretched between them, fueling the growing tension in the room. When he finally stood and took a few steps toward her, she was holding her arms tightly around her waist. He said her name again.

"I can't go back there," she said quietly and kept facing away. "I can't go back there with you."

"Back where?"

She shuddered. "To the crash. To that time. I'm trying to forget, not remember. I'm trying to get those days out of my head and——"

"Days?" he asked, cutting off her words. "What do you mean? How long were you in that car, Grace?"

She turned and faced him, eyes shining. She looked lost and he fought the urge to haul her into his arms. "Two days," she whispered.

Cameron stared at her. "You were trapped for two days? You and Richard?"

She nodded faintly. Very faintly. And Cameron's curiosity and instincts surged. Pieces of the puzzle fell into place. He recognized fear and grief in her haunted expression. And he knew that look from the years of police work and of dealing with victims of trauma.

"Richard was dead, wasn't he?"

"I said that already."

Cameron pressed on. "I mean he was dead when the car crashed. And you were alive?"

She took a second. "Yes."

"And there was nothing you could do for him, was there?"

Her lips trembled. "No."

Realization quickly dawned. She'd spent two days trapped inside a wrecked car with a dead man. No sweet wonder she was as closed up as a vault. The walls she'd erected around herself, the shadow of unhappiness in her eyes, her reluctance to let her family know the truth—it made perfect sense. "Grace." He said her name gently. "Has your counselor talked to you about post-traumatic stress disorder?"

She shuddered out a breath. "I'm not crazy."

"Of course you're not," he said and took a step closer. "But when someone has an experience like you've had it's quite normal for—"

"I'm perfectly fine," she said, cutting him off. "And I don't need analysis from your police officer's handbook."

Cameron took hold of her hand and urged her toward him. "Grace, I'm not analyzing you. I just wish you'd told me earlier."

"Why?" she asked, but didn't pull away. "So you can get inside my head and work me out?"

"So I could help you," he said gently.

"I don't need help. I'm not about to fall apart."

"Maybe you should," he suggested. "Maybe falling apart is exactly what you need."

She didn't move for a moment and uncertainty clouded her expression. Cameron remained still and waited. Her eyes filled with tears that slowly spilled over. Her skin looked pale in the lamplight. And she'd never seemed more beautiful. He wanted to soothe her, hold her, kiss her. But he checked himself.

"I can't. I have to fight it. I have to fight...you."

He touched her face. "No, you don't. We're not at war anymore."

"You don't understand—I need to stay strong," she said. "It's all I know."

"There's strength in admitting you're scared, Grace," he assured her and wiped the moisture from her cheek with his thumb. "And there can also be strength in tears. Resisting your grief and fear won't help you move on from the crash. It will only magnify the guilt you feel because you survived."

Grace choked back a sob. *How could he know that?* Months of guilt and anguish pressed between her shoulders. She dropped her head against his chest as his arms came around her.

"I was glad," she admitted as emotion tightened her throat so much she could barely swallow. Grace forced more words out. "I was happy and I shouldn't have been. I didn't have the right to be happy...not when Richard was...was gone."

Cameron stroked her back tenderly. "It would have been relief, Grace. And a perfectly rational reaction."

She shook her head against him. "No. I was *happy,* really happy." She shuddered as fresh tears burned her eyes. "We were trapped inside. I couldn't get out of my seat. Richard was...he was next to me and I knew he wasn't breathing and there was so much blood. But when I knew I was alive and not seriously hurt I started laughing hysterically and I couldn't stop and it—"

"That's not happiness, Grace," he insisted. "It was relief, like I said. You went through a traumatic experience." He grasped her chin, tilted her face and gently kissed her forehead. "You *should* be glad you survived. And thinking that doesn't make you a bad person."

More tears came, hard racking sobs that pushed up from deep inside her. She couldn't stop them. The tighter he held her, the more emotion came to the surface. For months she'd kept it all inside. Even with her therapist she'd held back, afraid to fully let her feelings show. Now, like never before, she felt like telling him everything.

When Cameron led her back to the sofa and sat down she followed and settled beside him. Without a word he turned her toward his chest and rested one hand over her hip, while the other stayed firmly on her shoulder.

"Grace, what happened during those two days, when you were stuck in the car?"

She wiped tears off her cheeks and looked at him. "The client we were to see lived in an isolated place. There was poor phone reception so we didn't know that the client was ill and had actually cancelled the meeting. Because of that, no one knew that we hadn't arrived for our appointment. We weren't reported missing until about thirty-six hours after the crash. It was Richard's wife who reported us missing when he hadn't called her the next day."

"And?" he prompted.

She shuddered. "It was a deserted road and a small animal had rushed out in front of us. Once we crashed, the car flipped onto its side and I couldn't open any of the doors to get out. And I couldn't find my phone so there was no way to contact anyone or call 911. So, I waited and just hoped that wild animals or dehydration wouldn't get me before I was found. And all that time Richard was…" She stopped and swallowed a heavy lump of emotion. "He was strapped in by the seatbelt and I was underneath. I couldn't climb over him. I couldn't do anything. And I kept thinking…why me? Why did I survive? If the car had landed a foot or so over, the passenger side would have hit the tree. But it didn't. It crushed the driver's side and the car rolled and it all happened so fast Richard didn't stand a chance." She sucked in a deep, painful breath. "He was a good man. His family grieved for him so much."

"That's to be expected."

Her shoulders grew heavy. "I know. And I know these things are random and happen and there's no way of controlling it…but still, I can't help wondering. In a split second someone lives and someone dies. There's really no sense to be made."

Cameron touched her hair and her heart contracted at his gentleness. "I think that every time I'm on duty and attend a motor vehicle accident. Your feelings are real, Grace. But if your friend died on impact there's nothing you could have done. It wasn't your fault."

Logically, Grace knew he was right. Her therapist had said it often enough. But the feelings lingered. Fresh tears filled her eyes and she blinked and more truths tumbled out.

"Richard's wife came to see me when I returned to work. She said she was collecting the rest of his things from his office, but I knew that wasn't the only reason." Grace took a long breath. "She stood in the doorway and stared at me... and somehow I knew what she was thinking. She looked around at my office, saw there weren't any photographs on my desk or anything in the room that might indicate that I meant something to someone, and I could feel her resentment. I felt such *guilt* in that moment that I couldn't speak. I couldn't talk about Richard, I couldn't express my sorrow for her loss. He was a man with a loving family and so much to live for, and I was just...I was...*me*—work-obsessed, closed off, friendless."

The truth was raw and painful and her whole body ached, inside and out.

"I don't think I've ever felt as alone as I did in those few minutes," she admitted with a sob. "An hour later I fell apart in front of a client and my boss made me take some leave and see a therapist. My treatment was to come home." She shrugged and didn't bother to wipe the tears from her cheeks this time.

"You don't need validation for surviving the crash, Grace. Not from your family, me or anyone else."

She couldn't pull back the agonized groan that escaped her lips. His insight both scared and soothed her. Her feelings were jumbled and when he moved closer the words she wanted to say somehow disappeared. His mouth hovered near hers. She pushed forward and their lips met, softly, because she wasn't sure she should do it. Part of her longed to kiss him over and over and try to erase the pain and guilt in her heart. And part of her wanted to run. Because she'd run from her feelings for Cameron since she was eighteen years old.

She pulled back and broke the contact of their lips. "I shouldn't have done that."

"I didn't mind."

She sighed heavily. "I know. And that's why I shouldn't have done it. I also shouldn't have told you what happened. It's my problem and—"

He kissed her hotly and the rest of her denials faded. Grace wasn't sure how long the kiss lasted. When he stopped she was breathless.

"Then why did you tell me?" he asked. "If for no other reason than you needed to talk about it to someone."

"Because you—"

"Does my wanting you frighten you that much?"

Her heart stilled. Had she ever really been wanted? By Dennis? By Erik? Had she really wanted them in return? A resounding *no* rang out in her head. She'd only wanted a career. Not love. Not sex. Not a home and family. Just work. And now, she was as vulnerable as she'd ever been, with the one man who could make her forget she had a life waiting for her back in New York.

"I can't," she admitted hollowly. "I just can't. Not with you."

His brown eyes absorbed her as he twirled strands of her hair between his fingers. Finally, he shifted in the seat. "You should get some sleep."

Grace stilled. "I'd like to stay here for a while, if that's okay?"

"Sure," he said and stood. "Good night."

As she watched him walk from the room, Grace knew that as confused and tired as she was, all she really wanted to do was fall into Cameron's strong arms and stay there for the night. And maybe longer.

## Chapter Nine

Cameron flipped on his back and stared at the ceiling. Sleep was out of the question. He managed to waste about an hour or so before he got up, pulled on jeans and a T-shirt and padded down the hall.

Grace was asleep on the sofa and he covered her with a knitted blanket hanging over the back of the love seat in the corner. She looked exhausted and he lingered for a moment, considering everything she'd told him. Without her secrets and frosty reserve she seemed achingly vulnerable and it pierced his heart.

He wanted her.

*He loved her.*

And she was so messed up he should ignore every feeling he had. Because he was going to get his heart smashed. Again. She was leaving in two weeks. She didn't want a relationship with him. She didn't want marriage or kids. She'd spelled it out many times.

*Dumb ass.*

He longed for the impossible.

She stirred and he quietly left the room and headed for the kitchen. He pulled a glass from the cupboard and filled it with water. *I need to chill out.* Not that he needed any more thinking time. He'd been thinking about Grace all his adult life. She was why he'd never settled, never made a commitment with any of the perfectly lovely women he'd dated.

*I just can't. Not with you.*

That was plain enough.

It should have worked like a bucket of cold water over his feelings, his longings and his libido.

"Oh—sorry. I didn't realize you were still awake."

He looked up. Grace stood in the doorway.

"Thirsty?" he asked.

She shook her head. "I didn't mean to disturb you."

"That's okay. I couldn't sleep."

She glanced at the clock on the wall which had just ticked past eleven o'clock. "I guess I crashed out for an hour or so."

"You must have needed it," he said and came around the counter.

Grace hesitated by the doorway. "Cameron," she said with a shaky breath. "I wanted to thank you for listening earlier. I've never really talked about the crash or Richard before."

"No problem."

"And about what I said…I meant…I meant that I…"

As her words trailed off he leaned against the counter and shrugged. "You can't force feelings Grace, I get that."

She shook her head. "That's not it."

Cameron's heart surged forward, battering against his chest. "Then what?"

"It's why I left," she said on a breath. "Why I couldn't be what you wanted back then. I knew you were getting serious and the plans I had didn't include Crystal Point or settling down."

"So you left for New York and didn't look back?"

"Yes," she replied. "And in two weeks I'll be going back there. You know that, right?"

"Sure."

"So, if anything happened it would—"

"Anything?" he prompted.

Cameron uncrossed his arms and pushed himself off the counter. As he moved the air between them shifted on some invisible axis. Hotter somehow, even though it was obviously cool outside. And thicker, like a gust of something sinfully seductive had blown into the room.

She sucked in a breath. "I want…I want…"

"You want what?"

Her green eyes glittered. "I want to…*feel.*"

Cameron kept his head. As beautiful as she was, as inviting as she was, he needed to be sure of her. "You know, you've had a pretty harrowing day. And bad days can make for impulsive decisions."

"I'm never impulsive."

"You were on the beach last weekend," he reminded her.

She shrugged a little. "So, despite what people think, I'm a normal woman with a normal woman's needs."

"I know you're a woman, Grace," he said quietly. "But today was hard—not only did Thomas almost die, you talked about the crash that almost took *your* life. When emotions come out like that, feelings can get…misdirected." He took her hand. "The thing is, if you want comfort—I can give you that. If you want sex—I can give you that, too. But tomorrow, I'll still be me. And you'll still be the same woman who wanted to get away from Crystal Point."

She moved closer. "Tomorrow isn't tonight. But if you don't want me I'll understand and—"

"Grace," he said, cutting her off. "Of course I want you." He ran his fingers through his hair. "I'm not made of stone. Do you think I haven't been imagining what it would be like to make love to you every minute of every day?"

She smiled. "Then make love to me. Please."

Cameron blinked twice and wondered if he were dreaming. She looked so beautiful. And startlingly vulnerable. He found some life in his legs and moved across the room.

"You're sure?" he asked.

She nodded.

He gripped her hand and she curled her fingers around his and turned, urging him forward and down the hall to her bedroom.

Once there she released him and stood beside the bed. Cameron's heart hammered. He'd imagined this moment countless times—even when they'd pretended to hate one another. And now he was with her, in her bedroom, standing barely a foot apart.

"But you're not sure about this, are you?" she asked and twisted her fingers together. Grace was nervous.

*So am I.*

"I'm sure," he replied and took her hand in his. "Only, I'm still me, like I said. I'm still a small-town police officer—and it's what I'll always—"

She reached up and placed two fingers against his mouth, cutting off his words. "I was eighteen and foolish when I said that. Who hasn't said stupid things in their life that they regret?"

She had a point. He regretted many of the things he'd said to Grace over the years. The digs, the antagonism— foolishness to hide behind so he didn't have to face his feelings for her, and the rejection he'd felt. But he wanted her so much. And right at that moment, the risk of getting his heart broken was worth it.

He took her hand and urged her forward, cupping the back of her neck with his other hand. "There's no going back once we do this, Grace."

"I know."

Without another word he drew her close and took her lips in a deep, drugging kiss. She groaned low in her throat and gripped his shoulders, holding on as breath and souls mingled. Kissing Grace was like nothing on earth.

Need for her spiked and his arms tightened around her waist, settling on her hips. Her sweatshirt fell off one shoulder and the bra strap went with it. He trailed kisses down her jaw and neck. The scent of her skin was powerful to his senses and he felt all the blood in his body rush to his groin.

*Go easy...go slow.*

She said his name and ran her fingers through his hair. Her eagerness spiked his desire. "Take this off," he muttered against her shoulder, tugging lightly at her sweatshirt.

"You first."

Obliging instantly, he released her for a second and pulled his T-shirt over his head and tossed it on the floor. Her palms came to his chest and the touch sent his blood soaring. He kissed her again, hungry for the taste of her. Her mouth opened and she rolled her tongue around his, softly at first, almost tentative and it made him smile.

Grace pulled back, all eyes and swollen lips. "You're laughing?"

"No," he said gently and grasped her chin. "Just thinking how good it feels to be with you like this."

She nodded and stepped back, then grabbed the hem of her sweatshirt and slipped the garment off in one fluid movement. Cameron watched, absorbed by the evocative look in her eyes. The white lace bra pushed her breasts upward and his hands tingled. He wanted to touch her breasts so much he ached. But she was calling the shots at that moment and he didn't mind one bit.

She discarded the top and rested her fingers on the waistband of her sweatpants. It was both excruciating and erotic to watch as she slowly slid the sweats past her hips and over her thighs. They dropped in a puddle at her feet and she pushed them out of the way with her foot. The white lace briefs were quite modest and unbelievably sexy.

She stepped back again and sat on the edge of the bed. When he moved toward her she pushed back farther onto the mattress. Cameron rested a knee on the bed and looked down at her lying against the white quilt. Her dark hair fanned wildly around her face. Her body was curved and toned, her skin smooth. A tiny diamond glittered from her pierced navel and seemed oddly at contrast with the controlled, serious woman he'd always believed her to be.

"You are so beautiful." Cameron moved beside her and grasped her shoulder. "And incredibly sexy," he said as he ran his fingertips down her arm.

"Really?" She took hold of his hand as he curved his palm over one hip. "Cameron," she said, suddenly too serious. "Just so you know...I'm not very good at this."

He stilled. "This?"

"This," she said again, quieter, like she had some terrible secret. "I'm not very responsive. I mean, I like the idea of... making love. But when I'm with someone I sort of shut down. I think there's something wrong with me. I'm only telling you because I don't want you to think it's something you've done. Or didn't do," she added quickly.

A feeling akin to pain pierced his chest. How could she possibly think that? "The suit?" he accused. "He said that? He said there was something wrong with you?"

She nodded. "And before that. Dennis said—"

"How about we don't worry what the suit or the doctor

or anyone else has said to you." He grabbed her hand and brought it to his lips. "Can you feel that?"

She nodded again.

He traced his tongue inside her palm. "And that?"

"Yes," she whispered.

"Do you trust me, Grace?"

Her breath caught in her throat. "I do."

"So, trust me now," he said quietly. "Trust this. Trust *us....*"

He looked into her eyes, saw her agreement and then kissed her. For a while, kissing was enough. She gave her mouth up to him, responding to each slant, every breath and each time he took her bottom lip between his. He threaded his hands through her beautiful hair, loving the way the wild curls got caught between his fingers.

The need to love her right, to pleasure her unselfishly, had never seemed more important. Her hands were on his chest and her soft caress burned through him. He kissed her and reached for the back of her bra, flicking the garment apart. He felt her smile beneath his mouth and then she shifted her shoulders free of the white lace.

He looked at her breasts, wanting nothing more to worship them...and more...worship her. Tonight. Forever. When he cupped one breast and closed his mouth over her nipple he thought he might die a slow, agonizing death. Pleasure and pain ripped through his middle, arrowing downward, making him so hard so quickly, he wondered if he would pass out.

He said her name against the luscious peak and groaned when she pushed toward him. Her hands were in his hair, over his shoulders, his neck, everywhere, like she couldn't get close enough, touch enough, feel enough. He caressed her skin, finding the places she liked. When his fingers reached the band on her briefs she stilled and drew in a sharp breath.

"Relax," he whispered against her mouth. "And trust me."

\* \* \*

Grace looked into his eyes and nodded with a hazy kind of surrender. She did trust him. Completely. More, she realized as he efficiently dispensed with her underwear, than any man she'd ever known. And for the first time in her life, without questioning why, she gave herself up to feel…to really feel… like she'd always longed for in her secret dreams.

His hands were magic over her skin, his mouth hot and demanding, yet also gentle as he coaxed response from her. She gave it willingly and wound her tongue around his as their kisses deepened, touching his chest, his strong, smooth shoulders. And she waited for what she suddenly craved, she waited for his intimate touch. None of her usual apprehension rose up—instead, Grace let go of her insecurities and fell apart in his arms.

He knew how to touch her, knew where, as though he'd been touching her forever, and beyond. While he stroked her, while his skillful fingers drew narcotic pleasure along her every nerve ending, he continued to kiss her mouth. He took her bottom lip between his teeth and suckled gently. When the tempo of her breathing changed he released her mouth and looked down into her face. His eyes were dark, clearly aroused, and she lost all her inhibitions beneath his penetrating stare. Grace spiraled, she flew, her blood fired as every part of her raced toward a shattering climax so intense, so wondrous, she couldn't stop herself from saying his name, over and over.

She came down slowly, breathing in tiny gasps of air, floating on a steady wave of aftershocks. Her eyes burned. No tears, she told herself. Not now.

"See," Cameron said quietly, kissing her jaw, her chin, and the delicate spot below her ear. "Nothing wrong with you at all."

The tears she'd tried to deny suddenly filled her eyes and

she blinked, desperate for him not to see them. Too late. He wiped the moisture from her cheek with his thumb.

So vulnerable, so exposed, Grace felt the rawness deep down to her bones.

"Sorry," she whispered and moved to turn her head away.

Cameron grasped her chin. "For what? Feeling pleasure?" He touched her bottom lip. "Don't ever be sorry for that, Grace."

"For being so emotional," she explained, hot with embarrassment. She was naked and exposed while he remained half-clothed.

"Making love is emotional." He rubbed her lip again. "Or at least, it should be."

He was right. And she wanted it to be that way. She also wanted his clothes off.

Grace moved her hands to the top snap on his jeans. "My turn," she said, pushing past her awkwardness. "Take these off."

It took barely seconds and finally he lay beside her, skin touching skin, arms entwined. In the dim lamplight his tanned body looked bronzed and amazing. Grace touched the soft hair on his chest with her fingernails. She felt his arousal press against her belly.

"Okay?" he asked and traced one finger along her arm.

She nodded and leaned toward him. "Kiss me."

For the next hour he did more than simply kiss her. Cameron kissed and stroked her, using his hands and mouth to drive her toward the pinnacle of pleasure once again. When his tongue dipped in her navel and played around with the tiny piercing she had there, Grace almost bucked off the bed. *Who would have thought...* He groaned low in his throat and offered encouragement when she touched him, kissed him, although there was nothing particularly practiced about her technique.

And then, when Grace thought she could crave nothing else, want nothing more, he passed her the condom he'd placed on the bedside table. She sheathed him quickly, if a little unsteadily, and waited, poised for his possession as he moved over her. He took his weight on his elbows and watched her.

*This is it.* Some faraway voice spoke to her. *This is what I've been waiting for. This night. This man. This feeling.* And as he entered her slowly, Grace knew a sense of completion she'd never experienced before. He stayed still for a moment and she remained lost in his eyes.

When he moved, Grace moved with him. When he kissed her, she kissed him back. When he smiled against her mouth, she returned the gesture. Two people, somehow fused by more than making love. The pace between them quickened. More need, more urgency, more passion, she thought, from some dreamy place, as her body began the throb with a heady longing once again. She linked her arms around him, holding on, kneading wanting fingers into his back. And finally, when they could take no more, they came together in a white-hot frenzy of release.

When it was over, when the pleasure receded and their breathing returned to something resembling normal, Cameron eased his weight off her and lay at her side.

He grabbed her hand and held it against his chest. "Still okay?"

Grace let out a breath. "Yes."

"No regrets?"

"Not yet," she replied honestly. "Thank you."

"For what?"

"For being so…" Her words trailed as an unusual lethargy seeped across her skin. "So sweet."

"Sweet?" He echoed but she knew he was smiling. "Damned with faint praise."

Grace shifted closer. "It's high praise, actually."

"Okay then." He sat up and swung his legs off the bed. "Back in a minute."

He left the room and Grace stretched her body. She closed her eyes, only to be roused a couple of minutes later when Cameron returned and quickly shuffled her underneath the covers before he got back into the bed.

He reached for her, wrapping her in his arms once he'd flicked off the bedside lamp. "Get some sleep, Grace."

Grace sighed contentedly and pressed herself into his chest, trailing her fingertips up and down his rib cage. She closed her eyes again and listened to the steady rhythm of his heart as she drifted off to sleep.

When she awoke the following morning, Grace was alone. The digital clock on the table read half past seven. She could hear movement around the cottage. A door closed and Jed's familiar whine echoed from the kitchen where he was clearly searching for food.

Footsteps came up the hallway moments later and Cameron rounded the doorway with a cup in his hand.

"Coffee?" he asked as he came into the room.

Grace pulled herself up, conscious to not let the sheet slip past her breasts. Silly, she supposed. He'd seen all of her there was to see. But she couldn't suppress the niggling anxiety that began to knock steadily behind her ribs.

"Lovely," she said as cheerfully as she could. Morning-afters were not her specialty.

But Cameron clearly had no problem with them, she realized when he sat on the edge of the bed and passed her the cup. Lots of practice, no doubt. That thought didn't go down well either. He looked casual and relaxed. He wore the jeans she'd practically ripped off with her teeth the night before and nothing else. The top snap was undone and she stole a glance at the line of soft hair arrowing downward from his belly button. Color rose up her collarbone and she quickly sipped the coffee. "Mmm, good. Thank you."

"I have to go into town this morning to pick up Pat and the kids," he said easily. "If they release Thomas it'll take two trips so I might be gone awhile. But later, we could do something together."

Grace looked at him over the rim of the cup. "Didn't we already?"

He smiled and Grace knew he was remembering how they'd made slow, seductive love again just before dawn broke. "I guess we did."

"What did you have in mind?" she asked, trying to push aside the images in her head and the memory of his kisses. "And does that mean we get the day off today?"

"For sure. You've earned it."

Her eyes popped wide. "I have?"

"For yesterday," he explained, grinning. "And Friday you worked hard. I was thinking we could take the horses out."

"Horses?" Her smile disappeared as she placed the cup on the bedside table. "I don't really do horses."

He shrugged and grinned. "Okay, what would you like to do instead? We could go into town and have lunch if you'd prefer that?"

Her smile returned. He was being very sweet and she decided to make an effort and expand her horizons. "Actually, horseback riding sounds like fun."

He looked skeptical of her sudden turnaround. "You're sure?"

"Positive."

He kissed her soundly. "Great. So, what about breakfast?"

Grace groaned. "Are you always so chipper in the morning?"

Cameron laughed and grabbed her free hand. "Depends what I've been doing the night before."

"Sex puts you in a good mood?"

He rubbed the underside of her wrist. "You put me in a good mood."

They both laughed out loud. "I do not. Most of the time we seem to be working out new ways to insult one another."

"I like this much better," he said and brought her hand to his lips and kissed her knuckles.

"Me, too."

He took a moment to respond. "And if I said I wanted more—would that send you running?"

More what? Sex? "I told you I don't do this casually."

His gaze narrowed. "And I do? Is that your implication?"

"Well, I—"

"Did it feel casual to you, Grace?"

She shook her head. "Not at all."

"Last night I asked you to trust *us,* Grace. Whatever you think of me, you must know I would never make love to you unless it was *real.*"

Did she know that? Is that why her heart hammered so loudly? *I'm afraid.* In the cold light of day, with passion abated and only truth between them, Grace was forced to examine what she knew was her own truth. Somehow, the lines had blurred. The antagonism had gone. The feigned dislike had disappeared. She'd made love with Cameron and had felt love in that moment. From him. From herself.

He smiled and then proceeded to make love to her all over again, wringing the last vestiges of response from her, driving Grace toward some place where only pleasure existed.

Pat and the kids returned midmorning. Thomas was being kept another night at the small community hospital, and according to his grandmother was doing remarkably well.

She remained in the kitchen with the older woman and Emily for a while, sharing tea and talking about the children.

They discussed the upcoming trail ride and Grace did her best to hide her nerves. But Pat wasn't fooled.

"You'll be fine," Pat assured her and tapped her hand. "Cameron won't let anything happen to you."

Grace warmed from head to toe. "I know."

It was well before lunch when Cameron came into the house. She hadn't seen him since he'd picked up Pat and the kids. Instead, he'd been outside tending to the animals with Dylan and doing some minor repairs on the paling fence near the chicken run. She wasn't sure if Pat sensed a change in their relationship. But Grace could feel it with every fiber in her body.

"Are you ready to go?" he asked when he appeared in the doorway.

Grace nodded. "Although I need to get my cap."

Pat moved across the kitchen and grabbed a hat off a peg near the door. "Take this," she offered. "Much better to keep the sun off your face."

Grace took the battered wide-brimmed hat which looked like one her sister-in-law, Callie, often wore. "Er—thanks."

By the time they reached the stables Grace was so nervous her hands were sweating. The horses, both tacked and tied up, seemed huge and ominous.

"The hat," he said, motioning to the object in her hand. "You actually need to put it on."

Grace looked at the hat. It was old and shabby and she had no inclination to put it on her freshly washed hair. In fact, she had become accustomed to her new, all-natural hairstyle. "Oh, I don't think—"

"Wear the hat." He took it from her and plonked it on her head. "I insist."

Grace caught his smile and was just about to playfully protest again when his phone rang. He answered the call and spoke for barely a minute. When he was done he was frowning.

"Something wrong?" she asked.

"Lauren."

His sister. "Is there a problem?"

He shrugged. "Nothing much. Come on, let's get going."

It took a few minutes, but Grace was finally in the saddle. It was one of the Western types, so at least she had a horn to hang on to. And she was pleased the horse appeared to have a calm temperament and good manners.

"I haven't done this for twenty years," she told him.

"You'll be fine," he assured her. "Just follow me."

Clearly an accomplished rider, he reined his mount to the left and headed through an open gate behind the stables and into a wide pasture. It was a picture-perfect late-autumn day. The sky was clear blue, the air crisp and clean. The ground was reasonably flat and grassy with the occasional outcrop of rock and thankfully Grace's horse followed Cameron's. After a few minutes she'd convinced herself to loosen up. And she liked watching him. As with everything he did, he looked relaxed and confident.

"Where did you learn to do this?" she asked as they steadily walked.

"My mother's folks owned a farm out west. I'd go there during school break."

How little she knew about him. A memory clicked in. "They're both gone now?"

"Yeah," he replied. "They died within a few weeks of one another. After fifty years of marriage they couldn't bear to be parted I guess."

It was a romantic notion. Fifty years together—as companions, lovers, friends, parents...what an incredible legacy to leave behind. It softened something inside her and being with Cameron got her thinking. He wanted her like she'd never been wanted before. He'd whispered words against her skin, drawn pleasure from every part of her and given her the confidence to let go of her inhibitions. And now, as she rode with him in the afternoon sunlight, for the first time in her life Grace wondered if she actually could have it all.

## Chapter Ten

"So, what did your sister want?" she asked, shifting her mind from images of them making love and imagining happily-ever-afters. Her question sounded impossibly nosy and she was surprised when he answered.

"Giving me a lecture."

Grace immediately tensed. Did his sister know they were together? Was that why Lauren had called her brother? The horse sensed her tension and responded by breaking into a trot. She caught her balance and rose from the saddle every second beat before collecting the reins and easing the gelding back.

Cameron was beside her in a flash. "Are you okay?" he asked and lightly grabbed one of her reins.

"I'm fine." Grace took a breath. "A lecture about what?"

He released the rein. "My mother wants to know if I'm going to the Jakowski family reunion."

Grace had a vague recollection that his entire extended

family got together every year. "Oh, right. It's tradition for you to all meet once a year?"

"Yep."

Grace tilted her hat back. "Well, it should be a good day."

"Maybe."

She pulled back fractionally on the reins. "Isn't it usually?"

He shrugged. "I haven't been for the past few years."

Grace eased the horse to a halt. Cameron took a few more paces to stop and then turned the toffee-colored gelding around. Head to head, the horses nuzzled one another.

She stared at him. "But isn't the day a big deal for your parents? And all your other relatives, like your grandparents and cousins and such?"

"I guess."

Grace took a deep breath. She sensed his energy changing. He didn't want to talk about it. However, she did. "Let's stop for a while," she suggested. "There's a spot over there near those trees. We can tie the horses up."

Without waiting for him she clicked the horse forward and trotted toward the trees. Once they were both dismounted she handed the reins to Cameron and waited for him to securely tether the animals.

She found a rock beneath the shade of a tree and watched as he retrieved two small water bottles from his saddlebag. Once he joined her she spoke.

"Tell me why you don't go. And tell me the truth."

Cameron didn't want to admit to anything. "It's complicated."

She took off her hat and raised her brows. "That sounds like something I'd say. You don't do complicated. So, 'fess up."

He smiled at her words. This was a new Grace. A little playful, even though she regarded him with serious eyes. He liked it a lot. But he wasn't quite ready to admit the truth.

"I'd rather not talk about it."

"Too bad," she shot back.

Cameron sucked in a frustrated breath. "Because it's a *Jakowski* family reunion."

She stared at him. "And?"

"And I'm not a... I'm not really a Jakowski."

It was the first time he'd said the words out loud. In the past he'd been asked the same question and always used excuses like work commitments, or lack of time. But he wouldn't lie to Grace.

And she asked another hard question. "Because you were adopted by Franciszek?"

Relentless, he thought and inhaled. "Yes."

"Do you actually believe he regards you as anything other than his real son?"

He shrugged. "I never said it was rational."

She grabbed his hand and Cameron felt the connection through to his blood. Her nails tapped on his palm. "You were what—three years old when he married your mother? So that's thirty-three years of being your father. Not that I'm an expert on parenting, but I don't imagine he'd be anything other than incredibly proud to call you his son."

He knew she was right...in his head. But the last time he'd attended the family reunion he'd realized he was the only one there not related by blood, aside from respective spouses. The extended Jakowski clan was large and traditionally Polish, where bloodlines and birthright were important. And that blood didn't flow through his veins. It was why he wanted his own family, his own children.

And Grace, he knew, did not.

"Like I said, not rational."

She linked their fingertips. "You know, you don't hold back telling me what I should do—my family not knowing about the accident as an example. So, here's a little of that back at you—you *should* go. Because they're your family and they love you. If that's not enough, then go out of respect for Franciszek, who loved you enough to want to call you his son and give you his name. And out of respect for the man you have become."

Shame hit him squarely between the shoulder blades. She was right. So right. He knew he hurt his parents by not attending. He had a sudden idea. "Would you go with me?"

"Go with you?" she echoed. "Like a...date?"

"Yeah...my date. My friend." *My girlfriend.* He felt about sixteen years old just thinking it.

She managed a wry smile. "I'll...think about it."

When he leaned forward and kissed her it took about five seconds for Grace's brain to kick in. He cupped the back of her neck as she returned the kiss, tasting her lips for the longest time. Finally they pulled apart. She was breathing hard, taking deep puffs into her lungs.

"Let's keep going," he suggested and pushed away the thoughts she had of lying down on the soft grass and making love with him. "The horses will get restless if we stay here."

She nodded, grabbed her hat and stood. Within minutes they were back in the saddle and headed east. They stayed out for a couple of hours, mostly walking through fields that belonged to an adjoining landowner.

When they got back to the farm she left the horse in his care and returned to the cottage.

Grace had blisters on top of blisters. Horseback riding. A great idea—*not*.

She ached all over and as she peeled off her jeans she grimaced at the red and angry blisters formed on the insides of her calves. She figured the ones on her behind would be worse. Just how was she supposed to rub the aloe vera there?

Pat had chopped off a leaf from the overgrown plant by the house when Grace had hobbled from the stables.

"Are you okay?"

Cameron stood in the doorway of her bedroom. His eyes briefly darted to the unmade bed before returning to her face. To his credit he didn't stare at her near-naked bottom half. Her sensible skin-colored briefs disguised little. She pushed the jeans aside with her feet. "Fine."

He nodded and looked like he was doing his best not to smile. "Need any h—"

"Fine," she muttered. "Like I said."

He pulled something from his back pocket and held it out to her. "Balm—for the sore spots," he explained. "Only use a little, it's pretty powerful stuff."

Grace took the tube. "Thanks."

Once he left she sank onto the bed. She needed thinking time.

They were lovers. Did lovers spend an afternoon riding horses, laughing together, enjoying one another's company? Did lovers attend family gatherings like the one he'd asked her to attend with him? Grace was more confused than ever. In the past she'd always been well into a relationship before having sex. Making love before making any kind of commitment. And her history of commitment was one of *noncommitment*.

Their differences seemed suddenly insurmountable. She had a life in New York…Cameron's life was clearly in Crystal Point. She was desperate to regain her edge again, to go back to work and be successful. Cameron wasn't career driven in the same way. She knew he liked being a police officer and was exceptionally good at it—but it didn't define him. And he wanted the kind of woman she could never be.

She showered, hoping to clear her thoughts, and then applied some balm before she changed into gray-and-pink sweats. Her hair seemed to have a life of its own and framed her face in a mass of curls. No makeup. All natural. It felt right in so many ways. And that was the core of her growing dilemma. Her two worlds were clashing. And she didn't know which one would claim her.

"Hungry?" Cameron asked when she walked into the kitchen.

He'd also showered and changed into loose-fitting jeans that sat low on his hips, and a white tank shirt. "Yes. What's on the menu?" she asked as her gaze lingered on his broad shoulders.

He held up a casserole dish. "Just have to heat it up. You could set the table."

She did the task quickly and grabbed sodas from the small refrigerator. As she moved around the room Grace was again struck by how normal it all felt. She couldn't remember ever experiencing such a strong sense of companionship with anyone before.

During dinner and the few hours that followed they talked, laughed and made out for a while on the small sofa. Grace relaxed in his arms as they watched television and sipped coffee. Afterward he took her to bed and made gentle love to her.

They planned to leave midafternoon Monday, which still gave them a couple of hours in the morning for Cameron to continue painting while she spent some study time with Emily. Cameron took Pat to the hospital to collect Thomas at nine o'clock, and while he was gone she and Emily abandoned the books and roped Dylan into helping them with the decorating. By the time Cameron returned she was rinsing out brushes by the back door.

"You're done?" he asked, staring down at her from the top step.

Grace craned her neck around. "I'm done."

"Good job. We'll leave after lunch if that's suits you?"

"Of course. I need to clean up and pack first."

By one o'clock Grace found herself deep in Pat's full arms. The older woman was returning to Crystal Point the following day with Emily and the other children. "Make sure you stay in touch. I know my granddaughter is thriving at her schoolwork with your help." Pat made her promise to stay connected. "It's been wonderful having you."

Grace blinked at the hotness in her eyes. In just days she'd become unexpectedly attached to the harried-looking woman and her grandchildren. "I will," she assured her. "Thank you for having me—I've enjoyed being here."

She said goodbye to the children, lingering with Thomas, who was still a little weak from his ordeal, but assured of a full recovery. She made a date with Emily for a brief lesson on Tuesday afternoon, mindful that she'd agreed to watch Noah's kids that evening. Jed lay on the backseat as Cameron stowed their bags in the trunk and then they were on their way. She watched as the kids waved frantically when they drove off and Grace swallowed the hard lump in her throat.

The return drive took a fraction over three hours. The familiar sight of the Pacific Ocean as Cameron crested the road heading into Crystal Point was unusually comforting to her. He pulled up outside the B and B. Five minutes later her bags were upstairs and they were staring at one another across the small lounge room.

"Everything okay?" Cameron asked perceptively.

Grace nodded. "Of course."

"Scott and Evie will be back next week, right?"

She nodded again. "Monday. I'm looking forward to seeing Evie."

He rubbed his hands together. "Well, I guess I'll talk to you soon."

The mood seemed too casual. Too polite. He wasn't suggesting they continue to see one another. He wasn't suggesting anything. In fact, he looked as though he couldn't get away from her quick enough. "Sure."

He left without another word.

Grace spent over an hour with Emily on Tuesday afternoon. They talked about the previous weekend and Thomas's accident. Emily told her Cameron had visited Pat that morning to check on them. She didn't respond to the information—and didn't admit that she hadn't heard from him at all since he'd dropped her off the day before. Once she was certain the teen had a study plan for the rest of the week, she showered, pulled on jeans, a collared pale blue T-shirt and navy zipped sweater and headed for Noah's house. She was surprised by how happy the kids were to see her, and then remembered the gifts she'd given them last time and was touched when Hayley made her promise to read the book that she said was now her favorite.

It also struck her how nice it was to be an aunt. She'd never really taken the time to get to know her brother's kids. Her trips back to Crystal Point were usually short and infrequent and she always brought work with her. This time was very different. So many new experiences were filling places in her heart—places she was only now prepared to admit were empty. Even the time she spent with Emily had its own reward. The teenager was doing so well with her studies and Grace knew she'd ace her upcoming exam. Thinking she had played a small part in that made her feel good about herself. And genuinely happy for Emily. She'd even made some inquiries about fashion design school for her.

"There's food in the refrigerator. And we shouldn't be too late," Noah told her. Dressed up in a suit her brother looked handsome, and she told him so. "Thanks for doing this."

"My pleasure," she said and straightened his tie. "Have fun."

Callie came into the living room, stopped and stared at her. "You know, your hair looks good like that."

She'd forgotten to straighten her hair that morning. "It's my holiday hair," she said and pushed her curls back. Once she was back in New York, once she was back in her apartment, everything would return to normal.

*Then why does this feel normal, too? Why did a weekend with Cameron and Pat and the kids feel like a glove that fit my hand perfectly?*

"The twins haven't been in the bath yet," Callie told her. "But they are under strict instructions to behave."

Bath? Right. How hard could it be? She put on a smile. "No problem. Enjoy the night."

"Thanks again," Noah said as he kissed her cheek and then quickly ushered his family outside.

Five minutes later the twins announced they were hungry for dinner and Grace was just about to herd them into the kitchen when the doorbell rang. She told the kids to stay in the living room and went to the front door.

Cameron stood on the threshold. "Hey."

Her stomach flipped over in that way she'd become used to whenever he was near. "What are you doing here?" she asked, letting him into the house.

He shrugged. "I got you into this babysitting gig," he said with a grin. "I thought you'd like some backup."

She couldn't help the smile that tugged at the corners of her mouth. Couldn't help remembering what had happened between them over the weekend. Couldn't help wanting more. Which made it one massive complication.

Grace nodded. "You prepare dinner and I'll get them into the tub."

He gave a lopsided grin. "Good luck."

"What does that mean?"

He chuckled and followed her into the living room. "Don't turn your back."

"My back? I don't under—"

"Uncle Cameron!"

The kids were clearly delighted to see him and when he swung Matthew high in the air the little boy laughed hysterically. Hayley wasn't about to be excluded and clamored for attention. He hauled them both in his arms for a moment and zoomed around the room making *vroom vroom* noises. Grace stood by the doorway. He really was remarkable with children and as she watched him an odd and unfamiliar feeling bunched down low in her belly.

Children had never figured in her life agenda.

*Love had never figured either.*

She sucked in a breath. *Love.* Impossible. She wasn't about to fall in love. Not in Crystal Point. And not with Cameron. It was just sex. A holiday romance at best. She'd been vulnerable and sought comfort in his arms. Only a fool would think it was more than that. Only a fool would want more.

And only a fool would be mad at him for not calling her for the past thirty-six hours.

"You know where the kitchen is," she said to him and then put on her best serious aunt face. "Come on, you two. Bath time."

They groaned as Cameron set them on their feet and raced around the room for a minute before she was able to usher them down the hallway. By the time she got them into the bath, washed, dried off and changed into pajamas, nearly an hour had passed. The kids had thrown water at her when she tussled with them about washing their hair and Matthew wailed about the soap in his eyes. At the end of it she was wet and short on patience.

"Everything all right in here?" Cameron asked from the doorway of the twins' bedroom.

"Everything's peachy," she lied and finished buttoning Matthew's pajama top. "How's dinner looking?"

"All set," he replied and held out his arms for Hayley. "How do my famous cheese-and-bacon hot dogs sound, kids?"

Her niece raced toward him and climbed up. "Yay, Uncle Cameron."

*Good old Uncle Cameron.* Grace set her teeth together. The man could obviously do no wrong. She smiled extra sweetly and by the look on his face he knew, damn him, that she was close to tossing a shoe in his direction. "Let's go."

"After you," he said and stepped into the hall so she could pass.

Despite her determination to not like his cooking, she had to admit the hot dogs were the most fabulous she'd ever tasted. They were so good, in fact, she ate two.

Later, once the kids had their fill, Cameron took them off to tuck them into bed with a book for half an hour before they had to go to sleep. It gave Grace a chance to clean up the kitchen and put on a pot of coffee.

He returned twenty minutes later, didn't look the least bit harried and she pushed back a stab of resentment. He did everything with a kind of casual ease she suddenly envied.

"Is it exhausting being good at everything?" she asked when he perched against the counter.

His expression narrowed. "Is that a dig, or a question?"

She poured coffee. "I'm not being snippy."

"Really?" He took the mug she offered. "You know, there's no angle to getting along with people. You just do it."

She raised a brow. "You mean *you* just do it."

"Well, it doesn't help that you've got a Back Off sign stamped on your forehead." He grinned and then drank some coffee. "You've handed things pretty well this past week. You certainly got along with Pat and the kids."

"Strangers aren't as complicated as family or…"

"Lovers?" he suggested when her words trailed off.

Grace looked into her mug. "I was going to say *friends*. But I guess we've changed those boundaries now."

He looked into her eyes. "Friends? I'm not sure we've ever been that, Grace. But we can try…if that's what you want."

The thing was, she wasn't sure what she wanted. They'd crossed a line and she wondered how she'd ever face him when she returned to Crystal Point in the future. What would happen when he married and had children? It's what he wanted. And even though those plans had never figured into her own life, Grace knew it would be painful to see him settled with a wife and children.

*Because…*

Because her feelings had somehow become muddled. What she wanted had never seemed so unclear. She looked at him and felt his stare through to the blood in her veins.

If only…

*If only I was a different kind of woman.*

"Grace?"

"Sometimes I wish…I wish things were different."

"Things?" he prompted and placed the mug on the table.

She drew in a shaky breath. "Me. I wish *I* was different."

He stilled. "Why?"

"Because then I wouldn't want to run so far away from you one moment, and run straight toward you the next."

Cameron fought the urge to haul her into his arms. Her admission hit him squarely in the chest. Her behavior confused him. No surprise there, he figured, as women had been confusing men since the dawn of time. He'd spent two days wondering if he'd made the biggest mistake of his life by making love with Grace. Because now he wanted her more than ever.

"I guess you need to decide which one you want to do more."

She stared at her feet. "That's not helping."

"Do you think I'm going to make this easy for you?"

She looked up. "I'd hoped you would."

"Not a chance."

"Even though we both know the odds of this working out are…are…" She stopped and quietly drew in some air. "I live in New York and you live here. And despite this…this attraction between us, I don't want what you want."

Cameron edged toward her. "How do you know what I want?"

"Because I just know," she said on a breath. "You want to settle down and have a family and I've never—"

"Never is a long time, Grace," he said, moving closer as he cut off her words.

She put down her mug and backed up against the counter. "You want me to be blunt? Here it is—I don't want children," she said and he heard the rattle in her voice. "And you do."

"Aren't you jumping the gun a bit, Grace?" he teased. "There's a whole lot of other stuff that comes before having babies."

"I know that it's—"

"Like marriage," he said quietly. "And spending more time together than one weekend."

He watched, fascinated as her cheeks bloomed with color.

"But I thought—"

"You thought what?" he asked, cutting her off. "That I want more from you? You're right, I do. But only if you want to give it. I can't help wondering why you are so determined to *not* have a baby?" he asked and looped a hand around her nape.

She met his gaze. "Because a baby and a career don't mix. And since my career would always come first, that's no way to raise a child. I don't have that built-in *baby* gene like Evie or my mother."

He rubbed her neck softly. "So, never?"

"Never. Like I said."

"Then I guess we're doomed," he said and kissed her.

She sighed against his mouth and moved closer. Cameron gently pushed her back against the counter and cradled her into the crook of his shoulder. She fit so perfectly and was made for his arms, but he held back the words he wanted to say.

*She's not ready...*

And there was no guarantee she ever would be.

"I'm gonna miss doing that," he said and trailed his mouth to her cheek. "A lot."

She trembled. "I have to go back to New York. I'm not staying here."

"So you said," he whispered against her ear.

"I meant it."

Cameron nuzzled her neck. "But you're here now."

She made a sound, half groan, half sigh. "You're trying to confuse me..."

"I'm not trying to do anything," he said and nibbled her lobe. "Other than make out a little." Cameron found her mouth again and kissed her soundly. "But since I'm on the night shift for the next few days I really have to get going," he said, and pulled back. "I'll see you Saturday, around eleven."

She shook her head. "Saturday?"

"We have a date, remember?"

"A date?"

"The Jakowski family reunion picnic," he said and figured he had to get away from her as quickly as possible. Otherwise he might be tempted to do a whole lot more than kiss her neck. "You said you'd come with me."

Her brows shot up. "I said I'd think about it."

He half smiled. "And?"

"And…it's probably not a good idea," she replied. "It might give the impression that we're…you know, sleeping together."

"We *are* sleeping together."

"Really?" She crossed her arms. "I don't know about you, but I've been sleeping alone this week."

Cameron tried not to laugh. She was mad at him. Good. At least she was feeling *something*. "Missing me, then?" He let the words hang in the air for a moment.

"Not at all."

Her resistance made him ache for her, "Sure you are," he said and grabbed his keys. "I'll see you Saturday, eleven o'clock."

She still looked like she wanted to bail on their plans, but she nodded. "Okay… Saturday."

Then he left.

On Saturday morning Cameron picked Grace up from the B and B. True to his word, he hadn't called her. It hadn't been easy. But he'd done some serious thinking.

She was leaving in a week and he was running out of time. He knew she was fighting it…fighting him. She didn't want babies. She didn't want a relationship. She didn't want to stay in Crystal Point.

And yet, they had an incredible connection. He felt it deep within his bones. It *was* the kind of connection that could last a lifetime…if only she would let it.

Grace wasn't exactly smiling when he pulled up. She got into the car and strapped on the seat belt.

"I thought you might have stood me up," he said.

"A deal is a deal."

"Still mad at me?"

She looked straight ahead. "Jerk."

He laughed. "Well, it promises to be an interesting day.

How are things going with you?" he asked. "Told your folks yet?"

"No," she replied. "But it's you we're here to work on today, remember?"

He remembered. Cameron had a knot in his stomach thinking about it. He would much rather take Grace home and make love to her all afternoon. "I remember."

She frowned and then her mouth was slowly drawn into a smile. "You could have called."

"But we're doomed, remember?"

She shifted in her seat. "I'm here now," she said, reminding him of his words a few days earlier. "And still here for another week."

"Does that mean you'll be wanting my attention?"

"Jerk," she said again and crossed her arms. "I've changed my mind about you. You're as impossible as always."

He grinned. He loved that about her. Loved that she had so much spirit.

When they arrived at the park he spotted his parents' sedan and knew his mother would hyperventilate once she saw him with Grace.

"Everything okay?" Grace asked as he walked around the back of the car.

She smiled and he was quickly bedazzled. "I'm good. Just waiting for my mother to ask what my intentions are."

"And what will you tell her when she does?"

Cameron's hand stilled on the picnic basket he was pulling from the backseat. His three weeks were nearly up and the words he wanted to say remained unspoken. But he knew he needed to get them out soon. He had a plan and he was going to stick to it. He grabbed the basket and closed the door. Grace had insisted they stop at the only organic deli in town and he watched as she organized the bewildered-looking girl behind the counter and pulled together a gourmet hamper.

He gazed at her as she collected a blanket and her bag, and admired how incredible she looked in a skirt, blouse and a bright red button-down sweater. His heart rate rose instantly.

"I'll tell her we've stopped hating one another," he said when she reached him.

"I never hated you," she said and stopped beside him. "Not really."

He touched her hand. It was their first touch in four long days. "No?"

"It was easier than facing the truth." She shrugged. "What can I say. I'm a coward."

Cameron squeezed her fingers. "You survived for two days alone and hurt in that car wreck. One thing you're not, Grace, is a coward."

She gave a brittle laugh. "It was only afterward that I fell apart."

"Which doesn't mean you lack courage."

Her eyes glittered and she pulled her hand away. "Yes, well…we should get going."

The reunion was in full force. About seventy relatives had turned up and tables topped with bright checkered clothes and crockery had been set up beneath a pair of giant trees. Away from the barbecues a group of children played and he spotted his father knee-deep into a game of Twister with a few of his great-nephews.

He saw his mother at one of the tables, sorting through plates and cutlery. She looked up as he approached and he knew the exact moment she realized Grace was at his side. Her surprised stare turned into a genuine wide smile.

She came around the table and hugged him close. "Good to see you here. Your dad will be pleased."

Guilt twinged between his shoulders. It had been four years since he'd shown his face at a Jakowski reunion. "Yeah. I brought—"

"Grace," his mother said, moving from him to take Grace's hand. "Wonderful to have you here with us. You look lovely as always."

"Thank you, Rennie."

All of the Preston siblings called Cameron's mother Rennie, rather than using the more traditional aunt label, which was often given to older, close family friends. "I believe you're looking after the B and B until Evie and Scott return from their honeymoon next week?"

"That's right."

"And Trevor?" Irene asked of Evie's sixteen-year-old son.

"He's staying with his grandparents up north for another week."

Cameron saw his mother's brows go up. "How lovely that they have a grandson to visit them."

He shook his head. "Two minutes."

Irene gave an innocent look. "What?"

"Two minutes before you pull out the no-grandchildren card." He smiled. "You're slipping, Mother."

He could see his mother's mind working in overdrive. Could see her mentally planning weddings and baby showers and happily-ever-afters. He placed the basket on the table and tried to ignore the sudden acceleration of his heartbeat. Because he'd imagined them, too. By the time Lauren sidled up beside him, his mother had ushered Grace toward an adjacent table of relatives and was introducing her to a few of his cousins and their spouses.

His sister pinched his arm. "Just checking that you haven't turned to stone."

He frowned. "What?"

Lauren's brows snapped up. "I couldn't believe my eyes. Of all the women I would ever expect you to be with, she isn't one of them."

Cameron held on to his temper. "She has a name. And I thought you liked the Prestons?"

Lauren shrugged and her blond hair bounced around her face. "I like Evie and Mary-Jayne. And Noah," she said, and then let out a breath. "And Grace, I suppose. Don't mind me. I wallow in self-pity a lot these days. It keeps me company."

"Sorry, kid," he said and rested an arm around her shoulders. "I know you've had it tough."

"That's still no excuse for being mean," Lauren said, then squeezed him back. "Even if I have always thought one look from those green eyes could turn a mortal man to stone."

He grinned. "She's not what you think."

Lauren's eyes glazed over. "People rarely are, I guess. But I thought you hated each other."

"Nope."

Cameron stayed at Lauren's side, but his gaze moved to Grace. As she mingled with his relatives he realized nothing fazed her. The boardroom, his bedroom…a park filled with Jakowskis. She was effortlessly confident, supremely adaptable and worked the crowd as though she had known everyone for years. But he'd seen the other Grace, too—the haunting, vulnerable woman who'd fallen apart in his arms.

"Whoa," Lauren said and tapped his shoulder. "That's a look I haven't seen before." She made a face. "You really do like her?"

"I really do like her."

*I love her.* And he figured his sister had probably worked that out, too.

## Chapter Eleven

Grace allowed herself to be paraded around on Irene's arm. After they'd done the rounds of most of the relatives and spent a few minutes talking with a somewhat breathless Franciszek, they headed back to their table.

"Do I have you to thank for getting Cameron here today?" Irene asked as she pulled lids off plastic containers filled with assortments of cold chicken, potato and green salads and delicious-looking coleslaw.

Grace smiled and pulled a tray of cheese and smoked ham from the basket they'd brought. "He wanted to be here."

"That's sweet," the older woman said. "Although not exactly true. I know my son. But I'm grateful to you for making him see sense." She sighed. "He thinks I don't know why he avoids coming. But I do."

"I'm not—"

"My husband loves him just as much as he loves Lauren."

Grace managed a smile. "I think he knows that."

"I hope so. Is Cameron hoping you'll distract me?" Irene asked and smiled. "You might encourage me instead." She paused and then quickly got straight to the point. "Are you dating again?"

Again? So she did know about their past relationship. "Not exactly."

"Sleeping together?"

Grace's skin burned and she dropped her gaze. "Well, I—"

"Your mother is my closest friend, Grace," Irene said quietly. "If you and my son are involved then I'd like to know about it."

"We're…just…" She shrugged helplessly. "I don't know what we are for sure."

Irene tapped her arm. "I know Cameron. And I know you. I hope it works out the way you both want."

*But we both want different things.*

When they sat down for lunch she was seated between Cameron and his uncle Henryk. Unsurprised to discover Cameron could speak Polish, Grace laughed as she stumbled over the pronunciation of words he tried to teach her. He placed a hand on her thigh under the table and didn't move it for the entire duration of the meal. The awareness between them had been building all morning and so had her need for him. His desire for her made her feel both safe and scared and connected to him in ways that had her heart beating madly.

Later, while Cameron walked off to speak with his father, Grace remained with Irene and Lauren and helped clear away the leftover food. She knew both women were curious about her relationship with Cameron. When Irene wandered back to the car to grab a wicker hamper, Lauren stepped beside her.

"So, you and Cameron, huh?"

Grace placed the lid on a half-eaten tub of pasta salad. "Am I in for an interrogation? If so, I already had one of those from Rennie."

Lauren raised both brows. "You're both of age. You can do what you like."

"But you don't approve?"

"I love my brother," Lauren said quietly. "And I wouldn't want to see him get attached to someone who's not going to hang around."

*Like you.*

The other woman didn't have to say it. Everyone knew her life was in New York.

Everyone knew she'd never settle for a life in Crystal Point.

"I don't want that either," she said and stacked the tub into a basket.

"I hope so," Lauren said, clearly acting protective of her only sibling. "I know we've never really gotten along. But for Cameron's sake we should probably make an—"

"I'll fold the tablecloths," Grace said, desperate to shut down the conversation. She looked around for Cameron and found he was on his way toward them. She drew in a relieved breath, grabbed the brightly colored cloth from the table and started folding.

He joined them and sidled up beside her. "Everything okay?"

Grace glanced at Lauren, who'd now moved to the other side of the table packing up picnic chairs. "Fine."

"I'll take you home when you're ready."

She glanced at her watch, saw that it was after four and figured there was little point in lingering. She certainly didn't want to answer any more questions from Lauren or Rennie. Grace nodded and he took a few minutes to say goodbye to his family while she finished packing. By the time they were back in the car and on their way to Crystal Point it was half past the hour.

He was quiet and she wondered about his mood. It was hard to tell. Their relationship had changed so much in the past two weeks. The old Cameron she knew and was prepared for. She'd always handled the insults and sarcasm. But now things were different.

When they pulled into the driveway at the B and B the silence between them was deafening. He grabbed the basket from the backseat and headed to the side of the house and toward the door that led to the private living area upstairs. The sensor light flicked on and she pulled out the keys. Once inside, he followed her up the stairs and into the kitchen and adjoining living area.

He placed the basket on the counter before spinning around to face her. He looked tense. Maybe angry.

"Is everything all right?" she asked quietly.

"Sure."

She twisted her hands together. "So, today wasn't too bad."

"You're right, it wasn't." He was unreadable, impenetrable. The only sign that he was feeling anything was the tiny pulse beating in his cheek.

"Would you like coffee?" she asked, desperate for conversation.

He moved across the room and hovered in the doorway. "No, thank you."

Inside the small room the tension between them escalated instantly. He returned her stare, blistering and intense, and so hot it almost burned through to her very soul.

Her breath caught as realization hit. It wasn't anger that held him from her, kept him distant. It was something else. Something she'd only glimpsed once before—the time when she'd been in the bathtub. Since then, every time he'd looked at her, touched her, kissed her, she'd felt his restraint. He'd always handled her gently, as though he sensed her lingering inhibitions. Every touch had been for her—her pleasure, her needs.

This, she thought as her blood pumped with urgent anticipation—this was desire, raw and powerful. This was need generated from long days apart. This was another level, another place, another kind of connection she'd never experienced before.

*He wants me.*

"Cameron...I—"

"Come here."

She stilled at the sound of his softly spoken command, felt the heat in the room rise up and sweep through to her bones. The only sounds were her heels clicking over the tiled floor as she stepped toward him.

He reached for her, moving one arm around her waist as he drew her close. "I've missed you." His mouth hovered an inch from hers. "So much."

"I've missed you, too."

He fisted a handful of her hair and tilted her head back. When he kissed her, hot and hard and deep, Grace pressed against him. Her blouse got crushed in the onslaught but she didn't care. All she felt was him...his hands, his mouth, his tongue demanding hers. She gave herself up, felt his surging need and matched it. Grace dug her hands into his shoulders as he swiveled around and trapped her against the door frame. She moaned low in her throat, wild with need and an aching hunger for him that boiled her blood. He managed to push her sweater off her shoulders in between kisses and toss it aside. Her blouse gave way beneath his fingers as buttons popped. She didn't care. She wanted his hands on her skin. She wanted him around her, over her, inside her.

Once the blouse was gone her bra was next. Cameron tugged at the straps and pushed them down over her arms. Her breasts rose up to meet his mouth and his hot breath against one nipple, then the other, drove her beyond coherent thought. Her skirt and briefs were quickly dispensed with and Grace gasped as he picked her up rested her against his hips. She wrapped her legs around him and rocked, felt his arousal and rocked again.

She waited while he snapped the top button and zipper on his chinos. Then he was inside her, plunging deep, taking her on a wild ride. Grace wasn't sure where he got the strength to hold her as they moved together, but with one hand braced against the door frame and the other around her hips, he supported both their weights. Pleasure built, skin burned on skin, and when it came she let herself go. Driving, aching, seeking the release she craved, Grace clung to him as they came together in a shattering wave of white-hot bliss.

It seemed an eternity before their breathing returned to normal. When he finally released her and set her on her feet, Grace realized that while she was completely naked, except for her bra settled around her waist, he was still fully clothed. He didn't release her, though. He tucked her head beneath his chin, steadying her with one arm, the other still rested against the door frame.

"Where's your bedroom?" he asked hoarsely after a moment.

Grace motioned down the hall and within a second he lifted her again and held her against his chest. Once in her bedroom he placed her gently by the foot of the big bed. She stayed perfectly still as he discarded his clothes. The lamplight dappled the hard contours of his shoulders and arms and she thought how she'd never seen a more beautiful man in her life. Longing rose up and hit her directly in the solar plexus.

Grace pressed against him. "Cameron…"

"I want to make love to you."

She sighed out a breath. "Isn't that what you just did?"

Cameron grasped her chin and tilted her head back. "That wasn't so much making love as it was my need for you."

"And mine for you," she admitted on a whisper, coloring hotly. "I've never done anything like that before."

He rubbed her cheek. "I'm sorry. I don't usually let that part of my anatomy do my thinking."

Grace bit her bottom lip and smiled. To be desired so completely, so urgently and with so much unabashed passion was highly erotic. For the first time in her life she completely rejoiced in her sexuality. He gifted her immeasurable pleasure and she suddenly longed to return that gift. She wanted him to feel what she felt—complete abandonment, total trust and mind-blowing ecstasy.

She pulled back and linked their fingertips. "Come with me," she urged and led him into the bathroom.

When she flicked on the jets of the double shower spray and pulled him into the open cubicle he raised both brows inquiringly. "What did you have in mind?"

Grace laughed, pushed him gently against the tiled wall and circled her palms over his pectorals. "Whatever I want," she said, kissing a trail from one small budded nipple to the other.

Laughter rumbled in his chest. "Throwing down the gauntlet, Grace?"

She nodded and kissed lower. He was already aroused, already hers to take. "And if I am?"

He raised his arms and braced against the wall. "Whatever you want," he invited softly.

Grace smiled and eagerly took up the challenge. Tenderness and desire transcended through her fingertips, her lips, and her tongue. He offered her moans of encouragement, and when he could take no more, when she felt his control slip, Grace gave him all she could. In that moment she had the power, the potency in her touch to bring him to his knees as release claimed him, and she held him through the pleasure, giving him her strength and the feelings that were in her heart.

* * *

Four hours later Cameron was in the small kitchen making scrambled eggs.

*Which look as scrambled as my brain at the moment.*

Grace sat on the other side of the counter on a stool, wrapped in a fluffy robe, sipping a glass of wine. With her hair mussed, her eyes a kind of hazy green and her lips the color of cherries, she looked delectable. She smiled at him over the rim of her glass.

"Pleased with yourself, are you?" he asked as he stirred the eggs.

A dreamy look washed over her face. "Hmm?" She shrugged and the robe opened, showing the hint of cleavage.

Cameron did his best to concentrate on the cooking and not her exposed skin. "You know exactly what I mean."

She smiled again, deep and alluring. "It's no secret to you that I've had a fairly repressed sex life." She put down her glass. "Until now."

It was quite the admission. "Why?"

She shrugged again. "Control, I guess. I could close off and only give the parts of myself I was certain wouldn't make me vulnerable."

Cameron pulled the eggs off the heat. "Being vulnerable isn't weakness, Grace."

"I'm starting to realize that."

He came around the counter, grabbed her hands and swiveled the stool ninety degrees. "Can you let go of your control long enough to think about your future?"

His heart pounded as he spoke. He'd had days to plan what he wanted to say to her. But the moment he'd picked her up that morning it confirmed what he wanted to do. What he'd planned to do since they'd returned from Burdon Creek.

"My future?" The tremor in her voice was unmistakable.

"Our future," he said and moved between her legs, pulling her close.

She drew in a long breath and tilted her head. "I don't understand what—"

"Grace," he said as his heart thundered and Cameron took as much air into his lungs as he could. "I've spent the past sixteen years denying what I feel and I—"

"Cameron, I think we should—"

He place two fingertips against her lips. "Let me finish," he said gently. "I have to say this, Grace. I've been working out ways to say this to you for the past week. For a long time I've been pretty casual about how I viewed relationships. I didn't allow myself to get seriously involved with anyone. I kidded myself that I didn't want anything permanent, or any woman to mean more to me than some good times and sex. But that's not really what I want."

She stared at him, unmoving.

"At Evie's wedding everything changed." He touched her cheek and ran a thumb along her jaw. "All those years of fighting and insults and antagonism…it was as though I'd woken up in a reality where none of that stuff existed. And now I want permanent, Grace. And I want it with you," he said, cradling her hips intimately. "These past couple of weeks I've felt an incredible connection with you. Tell me you felt that, too?"

"I did," she whispered. "I do."

His grip tightened. "Then let's not waste that feeling, Grace. A lifetime ago I let you go even though I knew it was the last thing I wanted. And before I had a chance to tell you how I really felt about you." His thumb moved over her cheek and he smiled. He stroked her face one more time before he reached into his pocket and withdrew a small box. "I love you, Grace. Marry me?"

The world tilted on an axis and Grace felt like she was falling. She didn't, though. He was there, in front of her, holding her against him. His brown eyes were dark and rich. He flicked the box open and Grace saw the most perfect ring, a brilliant white diamond surrounded by superbly cut emeralds.

"The green stones are the same color as your eyes," he said and watched her as she continued to stare at the box. When she didn't move he spoke again, slower this time. "But if you don't like it we can change the—"

"I like it," she said quickly and drew in a sharp breath. "I really do." Emotion clogged her throat. And the *yes* she wanted to say so much danced around in her head. "But... Cameron...I...I..."

He pulled back, suddenly pale as he put space between them. "Are you saying no?"

Grace wobbled on the stool and then slid to her feet. "No... Yes... I mean, I'm not saying... I'm just saying—"

"You're saying what?" he asked, cutting her off.

"It's just so unexpected," she said quickly. "So fast..."

"Fast? We've been dodging around this for years. I love you...I'd hoped you loved me back."

Grace pushed back her shoulders and slowly moved across to the living room and sat on the sofa. Cameron remained by the kitchen, a trillion miles away.

"Please, come and sit down," she said and tied the robe tighter.

He nodded, came across the room and sat beside her. Grace took a breath, the longest she could. She wanted to touch him. She wanted to feel the safety of his arms around her. Instead she stared at the jewelry box he still held in his left hand.

"I know how hard that must have been to say," she said quietly. "And if I wasn't leaving next week, things might be different. But I—"

"So we can make them different, can't we?"

Another breath. Another dose of steadying oxygen in her

blood. "How? I have a life in New York. And a career I can't simply discard."

He stayed silent for a moment, absorbing her words. "Okay...you have a career. We'll work around it."

She met his eyes. "How can we do that? Your life is here. My life is there. And we both want different things." Grace grabbed his hand and the jewelry box lay between their palms. They were connected by a ring that part of her desperately wanted, but another part of her knew she couldn't take. "We both know what kind of wife you want, Cameron. One who lives in Crystal Point, for starters. And one who wants to settle down and raise a family with you. That's not me. That won't ever be me." Emotion burned her eyes. "I'm sorry. But I've never pretended to be anything other than who I am. I just can't be that kind of woman."

Despite knowing he was getting exactly what he should have expected, Cameron felt like he'd been punched in the gut. He pulled air into his lungs. "And that's it?"

Her hand moved off his. "I know it's not what you want to hear."

Cameron jumped up and the ring he bought her rolled to his feet. He left it there. "No, it's not."

She looked at the small velvet box and picked it up, holding it for a moment before she placed it on the low glass table in front of her. "My career has always been all I am. And I have to go back and prove to myself that I can do it again. For the first time in months I feel strong enough to do my job properly. Please try to understand."

He did understand. She was rejecting him. Again.

"Ambition above all else?" he asked, pulling a tight rein on his hurt and disappointment.

"Of course not," she replied. "But I've not made any secret of that fact that I intended to go back."

Cameron experienced a strange pain in the middle of his chest. She'd made up her mind. She was leaving. He'd lost her. Again.

"And tonight, Grace? Is it your way of saying goodbye? Chuck in some last-minute hot sex before you pack your bags and leave everything behind?"

"I'm not that—"

"What?" he shot back abruptly, cutting her off. "Cold?"

She looked instantly wounded and Cameron's insides burned with a hollow pain. He didn't want to upset her... not intentionally...but he was angry and disappointed and plain old hurt.

"You think I'm cold?" she asked in a quiet voice. "After everything we've... After tonight and every other time we've been together?"

"Don't confuse sex and love, Grace."

She stood up quickly. "What do you want me to say to you? That I'm torn...of course I am. This is the hardest decision I've ever had to make."

Annoyance began to weave down his spine. "Really? It seems fairly cut-and-dried."

She wrapped her arms around herself. "I didn't lie to you. I didn't make any promises. You know how I feel about marriage and children. I've worked hard to get the career I wanted. And now...now I have to prove that I can do it again without falling apart like I did after the accident." She sucked in a long, heavy breath. "I don't expect you to understand... you've never failed at anything."

*I've failed to get your love.*

"Of course I have," he said roughly.

"I mean you've never failed to be anything other than your-self," she said tremulously. "Last weekend with Pat and her grandchildren, I really saw you for the first time. I saw that you're funny and charming and incredible with kids and so unbelievably comfortable in your own skin. Wherever you go, you belong."

Cameron stilled. "I'm not sure what that has to do with you turning down my proposal."

"Everything. Nothing. It's just that you know who you are. And I'm a slightly neurotic, overachieving control freak who has never really belonged anywhere except in the life I've made in New York. Whenever I come back here it reminds me of how different I am from everyone else. Most of my life I've felt as though I have been stuck in between worlds."

He knew that about her and his heart lurched. "Then, how about we meet somewhere in the middle?"

She took a shuddering breath. "How can we? In the middle there's an ocean."

"It's just geography, Grace."

"It's more than that," she refuted. "It's about you being an important part of this community. And the kids like Dylan and Emily—they need you. I could never ask you to change or give up being part of that. Just like I can't change what defines me."

Cameron took four steps forward and reached her. He grasped her shoulders and molded the bones beneath his hands. He wanted to kiss sense into her. He wanted to love her until they weren't sure where she began and he ended.

"That's a cop-out, Grace. This isn't about the job or anything other than the fact you're scared to death to really feel something for someone. That's why every relationship you've had has been lukewarm. You chose the doctor and the suit because they didn't threaten your little safe world where you don't have to let yourself be seen for who you really are."

The truth hit Cameron with lightning force.

"I get it now," he said, releasing her. She shuffled back slightly. "I finally get why you came back. It's not about the car crash or your friend's death or because a therapist told you to spend time with your family. You simply don't want anyone to work out that you're not perfect. But now you've regrouped, right? You have your strength back—you've faced what happened in the accident and you want to dive straight back into that life. And by doing that you can once again turn your back on this place and everyone in it."

"I didn't turn my back on Crystal Point," she snapped, emotion bared in her eyes. "I was *sent* away."

He stilled. "What?"

"I was sent away," she whispered this time as she sank back onto the sofa. "To school."

"School? You mean—"

"I mean boarding school," she said, cutting him off. "I mean to a place where I didn't know anyone and where I was put in a class higher than my age because I was considered too smart, too advanced for my normal grade. A class where I was first tormented and then ignored for being younger and smarter…and different. And I'd come home for holidays and my family would all be here—this fabulous tight-knit unit— a unit I wasn't really part of. I was told how lucky I was to be getting such an amazing education. And they were right. I did get the best education possible." Tears glittered on her lids. "But when school was over and I came back I felt so out of place…so distant. That's why I couldn't stay."

The question he'd pondered a thousand times came out. "So it wasn't because of us?"

"No." She shook her head. "It was never about that. In so many ways you were the only reason I wanted to stay." She took a long, steadying breath. "But I knew you were getting serious and I got scared."

"Scared of what?" His insides crunched. "Of falling in love?"

"Of failing to be…more," she admitted unsteadily. "Of not living up to the expectations of my parents, my teachers…

and even myself. I had to live the life that had been planned for me. If I didn't, it meant it would have been a waste to send me to that expensive school. And I couldn't do that to my parents. But when I came back…"

He knew what she meant. "I got in the way?"

She shrugged. "I left quickly because I didn't want to get in any deeper."

His back straightened. "And still don't, clearly."

She held the velvet box in both her hands. "Please don't be like this. We can have tonight…tomorrow…"

"You know," he said quietly, resignedly, "I've pretty much loved you since you were sixteen years old. But I'd just joined the police force and I knew you weren't ready for a relationship. So I waited a couple of years—waited until you were old enough. When you came back from school and we started dating I thought it would lead to a life together. But you told me then that nothing would keep you in Crystal Point—especially not a small-town police officer. So I guess things haven't changed all that much." He took a deep breath and tried to not think about how much he ached inside. "Goodbye, Grace."

Without another word he turned around and walked out of the room. And out of her life.

## Chapter Twelve

When Evie and Scott arrived home on Monday, Grace heaved a sigh of relief.

Her flight back to New York was booked and although she was glad to have a few more days to spend with her sister, she also wanted to go home. *And New York is my home.*

She thought Evie looked exhausted and told her so. They sat together in the kitchen, sipping the peach iced tea her sister had begged for.

"I'm fine, honestly," Evie insisted and patted her bulging belly. "Just tired from the trip home. I did nothing but relax and get pampered by my lovely husband while we were away."

"You've popped out," Grace said as she looked at her sister's stomach. "And still a month to go."

"Three weeks," Evie replied. "I wish you were staying until then."

Grace drank some tea. "I have to get back to work. So, tell me about the honeymoon."

Evie grinned. "Everything?"

"Well, not *everything*."

Her sister laughed. "It was romantic in a mostly non-amorous kind of way." Evie rubbed her palms across her abdomen. "What about you? What did you get up to while we were away?"

*I made love with Cameron Jakowski. Again and again. Oh, and I got a marriage proposal, too.*

"Not much," she lied then explained about babysitting Noah's kids and tutoring Emily.

"Babysitting?" Evie's steeply arched brows rose significantly. "Really?"

"Don't look so surprised."

Evie smiled. "I'm delighted, not surprised. The twins are adorable. Notorious at dinner and bath time, though."

"Mmm…well, I had a little help."

"Help?"

Grace drew in a breath. "Cameron stopped by. He cooked dinner while I was on bath duty."

"Cameron did?" Evie's eyebrows went up again. "And?"

Grace shrugged as the weight of her suddenly complicated life pushed down heavily on her shoulders. "And we had dinner and then he left."

"That's not what I meant. What else has been going on with you two?" her sister asked with way too much intuition. "And don't bother denying it. After what happened at the wedding I wouldn't be surprised if—"

"I slept with him."

Evie's green eyes almost popped out of her head. "Oh—I see. And what else?"

She took a few seconds before she told her sister of the weekend at Burdon Creek, Thomas's accident and briefly mentioned how she and Cameron had become close.

"But why did you agree to go in the first place?" Evie asked.

She wasn't about to admit to Cameron's little bit of blackmail. "To help Emily."

Her sister clearly wasn't convinced. "Another thing I don't understand. Since when have you been a math tutor?"

Grace met her sister's gaze. "She needed help to pass a makeup exam. I'm good with numbers."

"I know that. You're the smartest person I've ever met. But you don't usually get...involved...with what other people are doing."

Now Grace raised a brow. "Is that a nice way of saying I'm a self-absorbed neurotic with little time for anyone other than myself?"

Evie smiled. "Well, I might not put it exactly that way."

"But the gist is the same? Yes, I know what I am. I know what people think."

Evie smiled again and drank some tea. "Well, who cares what others think. I love you for who you are. We all do."

Grace swallowed a thick lump in her throat. Shame and guilt pressed down on her shoulders. She felt like such a coward. She'd returned to Crystal Point and then run from the truth. As she had done over and over. If she was to be with her family and try to heal the disconnect she'd felt most of her life, then she needed to really *be* with them. She needed to let them in and admit she was scared and vulnerable and hurting.

She needed to tell them about the accident.

Cameron was right. Thinking about him brought a deep, hollow pain to her chest. His words resonated in her head over and over.

*I love you, Grace. Marry me.*

He loved her. It was the first time a man had ever said that to her. And the first time she'd ever wanted to say it back.

"What?"

Evie again, looking way too intuitive. Her sister could be relentless when she wanted to know something. "It's nothing." She took a deep breath. "I'd like to go to our parents' tomorrow night. There's something I need to tell you all."

Then she could go home.

"I hear she's leaving next week."

Cameron sat in the kitchen of his parents' house. His mother stood on the other side of the granite counter, looking at him over the rim of her reading glasses. Irene Jakowski always got straight to the point.

"So I believe."

"And you're letting her go?"

He ignored the jabbing pain at his temple. "Let's not do this."

"I didn't raise a quitter. I raised someone who became the kind of man who goes after what he wants."

*Until I got my heart crushed.*

"I can't make her feel something she doesn't," he said flatly and stared into the coffee mug in front of him.

Irene tutted impatiently. "If you want her you should fight for her."

"I also can't fight against her ambition," he replied and pushed the mug aside. "She's made it pretty clear what's important in her life."

"Cameron," his mother said, gently this time. "The Grace I saw at the picnic didn't seem too interested in her career. She couldn't keep her eyes off you. You're made for one another—you always were. Besides," Irene's eyes grew wide and she smiled. "I want grandchildren. With Evie's baby coming soon, Barbara will have six little angels and I don't have any. Soon I'll have nothing to talk about with my best friend."

Cameron smiled at his mother's sense of drama. "I didn't realize you were so competitive with Barbara Preston."

"Of course I am," she replied with a laugh. "What else do you think we want to talk about? Kids and grandkids are our staple diet of conversation. At least, it would be if you decided to settle down and supply me with some."

"Maybe you should try your luck with Lauren?"

"Hah," his mother scoffed. "Your sister has convinced herself she's a man-hater after that fiasco with what's-his-name. You, on the other hand, have an opportunity to be with a perfectly lovely girl who just happens to be the daughter of my best friend."

"Since when did you become the president of Grace's fan club?" he asked, trying to diffuse his mother's enthusiasm.

"Since I realized that you're in love with her."

He wasn't about to deny it. Irene Jakowski could see a lie through thick fog. "She's made her choice."

She took a breath. "And when did you become so black-and-white? You negotiate and work through problems every day in your job with those troubled kids you help. You don't give up on them—you don't give up on anyone. What about Dylan? Isn't he another example of keeping faith in what you believe? You wanted to help him and you did. You helped that entire family get back together. Don't the same rules apply in your own life?"

Her point had biting accuracy. "It's not the same thing."

Irene took off her glasses. "Oh, I see…bruised that monumental ego of yours, did she?"

"I don't see what—"

"You're as bad as your father. Did you know he dithered around for months before he asked me out and when I said I had plans he didn't bother to ask me again? I waited three weeks and then I asked him. Then I stood him up just to make a point. He got mad for about two days and then came back groveling. And he proposed marriage three times before I finally accepted him. Good thing, too."

"Is there a point to this?"

"My point," she said slowly, "is that women, even the most complex women, like to be wooed. Chased, pursued...call it whatever you like."

"And if she turns me down again?"

Irene grinned. "Go woo some more."

Cameron laughed for the first time that week. Irene Jakowski always said what she thought. Woo her? But he knew his mother was right. He had quit. Grace had announced her intention and he'd bailed, he'd walked off to lick his wounds in private.

*Fat chance of that in this family.*

He wanted to see her again. He wanted to hold her again. But he knew Grace...he knew the more he pushed the more she would resist.

"She's going back to New York," he said flatly.

"So, follow her."

Cameron stood and pushed the chair out. "I have to go," he said and grabbed his keys. "Thanks for the coffee." His kissed his mother goodbye and left.

Grace was incredibly touched by the support she got from her family when she told them about the accident, Richard's death and her ensuing breakdown. They sat quietly and listened as she spoke of the two days she was trapped inside the car and the fear that she would die before she was found.

"Why didn't you say something earlier?" It was Noah, her most practical sibling, who spoke.

"At first I was in shock about what had happened. And then...I was embarrassed that I'd fallen apart," she admitted and looked up from her spot on the big sofa. "Anyway, I apologize for shutting everyone out."

"Grace," her mother said and grasped her hand, patting it gently. "Even though you live thousands of miles away, you're still very much a part of this family. If you had called we would have been there for you."

Of course they would have. In her heart she knew that. But the feelings of disconnect she had from when she was sent to boarding school had caused her to close up like a vault. But right now, more than ever before, Grace knew she was loved. Everything Cameron had said was true. Grace could have wept. "I know," she said and managed a tight smile. "And thank you for understanding."

Except when she drove Evie back to the B and B, she couldn't miss the deliberate silence from her sister.

"Okay," Grace said as she pulled into the driveway and turned off the engine. "Say what's on your mind."

"Is there any point?" Evie asked and let out an exasperated breath as she unclipped her seat belt. "I can't quite believe you, Grace. Maybe our parents and Noah and M.J. were too stunned to say anything back at the house—but I'm saying it now—what gave you the right to exclude us so deliberately? You could have been killed. One of us should have been there—heck, we *all* would have been there if you'd only said something. A phone call. Even an email. Would that have been so difficult?"

"No," she replied softly. "You have every right to be angry."

Evie touched her arm. "I'm not angry. I'm…hurt. Don't do it again, Grace. Don't treat us like we don't matter."

Grace was about to apologize again when Evie winced. "What is it?"

"Nothing," her sister assured her and then touched her belly. "Only, I'm thinking the backache I've had today isn't backache."

"What do you—"

"I think I'm going into labor," Evie said on a rush of sharp breath. "You might want to go inside and tell my husband. And also tell him not to forget my bag," she added.

Grace was out of the car with lightning speed.

Sure enough, Evie did go into early labor. Grace stayed at the hospital through the night and was the first person to be told that her sister had given birth to a healthy baby girl.

Evie's husband, Scott, emerged from the birthing room to give her the news.

"They're fine," he said and ran a weary hand though his hair. "The baby is three weeks early, and she's...she's..." He stalled and took a deep breath. "Perfect."

"Congratulations," Grace said and found herself in the middle of a huge bear hug.

She didn't pull away. The old Grace would have balked at hugging anyone, let alone her brother-in-law. But she'd changed. Her prickles were...well, less prickly.

The ice princess had finally begun to thaw.

She left the hospital and headed back to the B and B to shower and change and give the new parents some time with their baby. But that afternoon she returned for a visit with her sister and took only minutes to be persuaded to hold the baby, who had been named Rebecca.

"She's so beautiful, Evie," she said, holding baby Rebecca close. A tiny tuft of dark hair stuck out above the top of her soft pink wrap and Grace touched her head gently.

Evie sighed contentedly and pushed back against the pillows. "I know. I can't believe she's finally here."

"And there were no complications during the birth?"

"Not one. She was eager to come into the world. Although I'd forgotten how tiring the whole thing can be. It's been sixteen years since I had Trevor."

Grace looked at her niece and smiled warmly. "Well, you did great. And Scott?"

"Poor darling." Evie's face lit up. "I sent him home to get some sleep. He's mesmerized by how perfect she is and has been staring at her for most of the day."

"He's a first-time father so I guess that's to be expected." Grace glanced at her sister and smiled. "It's really good to see you so happy."

Evie nodded and adjusted the front of her nightgown. "What about you? Do you truly believe going back to New York will make *you* happy?"

With her emotions bubbling at the surface the last thing Grace wanted to do was break down when Evie was experiencing so much joy. She put on the stiffest face she had. "It's where I live."

"That's not exactly an answer. Is it what you want?"

*What I want?* Grace didn't know. Holding the baby brought up so many feelings, so many longings. Her womb was doing a whole lot of uncharacteristic backflips and she suddenly found herself doing the unthinkable—actually imagining having Cameron's baby. The very notion brought heat to the back of her eyes.

"I wouldn't be doing it if I didn't think it was for the best."

Evie's mouth twisted. "I know you better than that. What exactly happened between the two of you?" her sister asked. "And don't just tell me you slept with him. There's more, I know it."

Grace touched Rebecca's face and marveled at the softness of her skin. She drew in a shaky breath and told her sister the truth. "He proposed."

Evie's huge green eyes bulged. "Cameron asked you to marry him?"

"Yes."

"And what did you say?"

Grace pushed back the emotion in her throat. "I said I was going back to New York."

"You turned him down?"

"I…guess I did." The pain of the words struck deep and Grace gathered her composure. "We can't have a relationship when we live in different countries, let alone a marriage."

"You could stay," Evie suggested. "Or you could ask him to go with you."

Grace didn't bother to hide her surprise. "His life is here."

"And yours is in New York? Yeah, yeah, I get that. I just don't understand why there can't be a middle road."

"Because…because there just can't. Cameron's life is in Crystal Point—his job, all the work his does with kids… I would never ask him to change who he is."

"And you won't change for him?"

She shrugged.

"Do you really hate Crystal Point that much?" Evie asked.

"I don't hate it," she replied quickly. "I just don't…fit in."

"Look at you," her sister said gently. "You're holding your niece like she is the most precious thing in the world. And for the past two weeks you've been running the B and B, baby-sitting Noah's kids and helping a young girl pass her exams. Does that paint a picture of someone who doesn't *fit in*?" Evie sighed. "You know, love is sometimes about compromise. You do love him, right?"

Grace pushed back tears and looked up, denial hanging on the edge of her tongue.

Evie's gaze narrowed. "Well, even if you won't admit it, I'll bet my boots you do."

Her gaze dropped immediately. "You know I—"

"Don't let anyone know what you're feeling…ever?"

The old Grace would have jumped all over her sister's words. But Evie was so right it hurt through to her bones. "I guess I don't," she admitted, thinking about the small velvet box in her handbag. She'd carried the ring with her since the night he'd asked her to marry him. Sometimes she opened the box to look at it, never quite having the courage to put the ring on her finger—afraid that if she did she would be forever changed.

"Like I said," Evie continued, "compromise. And sometimes one has to give and one has to take. It's not a competition, Grace, I mean to see who has to change the most…it's just the way it is. When Scott moved his life from California to Crystal Point he did it with an open heart. He did it because he *loved* me. And I am grateful for that every single day."

Grace touched the baby's soft hair. "But you had this beautiful girl on the way," she reminded Evie. "That's a big incentive for anyone."

"Love is enough, Grace. You just have to let yourself believe it."

*I'm not that brave—I wish I was.* Grace snuggled Rebecca against her chest and inhaled the sweet baby smell. She was a wondrous thing and she couldn't get enough of her soft hair and rosebud mouth. All her adult life she'd insisted that children weren't in her future. And now, as she held the newborn infant, Grace experienced a longing so deep and so acute her heart actually ached.

There was a brief knock on the door and Evie invited whoever it was to enter.

Grace almost hyperventilated when the door swung open and Cameron strode across the threshold. He stopped when he saw her and the flowers in his hand dropped to his side. He looked at Grace and then the baby she held in her arms.

The room spun momentarily. Her breath caught, making a sharp sound which echoed around the walls. Grace's heart surged. She hadn't seen him in what seemed like an eternity. In that time she'd experienced every emotion possible—from despair to anger and then a deep wrenching pain. And as he watched her with blistering intensity all of those sensations pulsed through her blood. Time stalled, drawing them both into a moment of acute awareness. With the baby held against her, Grace knew what he was thinking.

*This could be our child one day.*

A hollow ache rushed through to her bones. Her womb rolled, taunting her with the possibility of what *could* be. Like a speedy camera she saw it all so clearly—the home, the children and the happiness she'd always been afraid to want.

"Hey, Evie," he said, breaking the contact between them as he walked toward her sister, kissed her cheek affectionately and handed her the flowers. "Congratulations on your new addition."

Evie was appropriately grateful and glanced at Grace. United in loyalty, she recognized her sister's questioning look. Grace forced tears back and concentrated on the baby while Cameron and Evie spoke. She couldn't look at him. She was raw. If he said a word to her Grace knew she could break down and cry. And that wasn't an option. Not in front of Evie. And not in front of him.

Dressed in uniform, he'd obviously come straight from work. He looked so attractive and she was struck with images of how she'd often imagined stripping his blues off.

She stiffened when he approached and admired the baby from barely two feet away. The familiarity of him assailed her senses. His hair that she loved running her fingers through. His broad shoulders and arms which had somehow become a safe haven. Everything about Cameron made her want… made her need. She took a steadying breath as she stood.

"Cute kid," he said easily. But Grace wasn't fooled. His shoulders were tight, his jaw rigid. She knew he was hanging by the same thread she was. The temptation to run into his arms became a powerful force and it took all her will to keep a rein on her emotions.

Grace had placed Rebecca in her mobile crib when Evie spoke again.

"Would you like to hold her?" her sister asked Cameron.

His hand immediately rested on the pistol holstered at his hip. "Not while I'm wearing this," he said evenly. "I'll wait until she's home."

Evie nodded. "Well, I think I might take a little walk," she announced suddenly. "I need to stretch my legs. Look after Grace and my angel for a few minutes, will you, Cameron? I'll be back soon."

Grace watched as Evie shuffled off the bed, touched the sleeping baby on the cheek for a moment and then quietly left the room.

"That was subtle," he said once the door closed.

Grace swiveled softly on her heels. "You know Evie."

He raised both brows inquiringly. "You told her about us?" he asked. "I'm surprised."

Grace shrugged and moved across the room to stand near the window. "She's my sister. I tell her things."

He looked instantly skeptical. "You didn't tell her about the accident until yesterday, though, did you?"

"You know about that?"

"Your mother called mine. Mine called me."

Grace shrugged. "Well, everyone knows now, so no more secrets." From the window she spotted a view of the neighboring parklands and tried to concentrate on the scene and not think about how messed up her thoughts were.

Silence stretched like elastic.

"Do you know what I thought when I came into this room and saw you holding the baby?"

She didn't turn. Didn't move. Rebecca's soft breathing was all she heard. And the dreadful silence that grew in decibels with every passing second. She knew exactly what he'd thought. Because she'd thought it, too.

Cameron spoke again. "I thought how beautiful you looked holding the baby. And then I wondered how could I get you to stay? How could I get you to change your mind and give this…give us, a chance?"

Grace turned around and faced him. "You can't."

"I know, Grace," he said, keeping his voice low.

Her heart lurched forward. But she wouldn't break. "I'd like us to still be…friends."

"Friends? You're kidding, right? Since when have we ever really been friends?"

She drew in a shaky breath. "We could try," she whispered.

Cameron stepped toward her. He reached up and touched her cheek. "I don't want to be your friend, Grace. I want to be your lover and your husband and the father of your children. I want you to be the first person I see when I wake up in the morning. I want it all, as scary as that sounds to you. But that's what love is, Grace…having it all, wanting it all."

She nodded, although she wasn't sure how. "Cameron, I—"

"But I know that's not what you want."

Grace closed her eyes. It would be easy to fall under the spell of his gentle touch, his comforting voice. She opened her eyes again when he released her and met his gaze head-on as he stepped back. The growing distance quickly pulled them apart.

"I want…" Her voice cracked. *Like my heart is cracking.* "A part of me…a part of me does want those things." She looked at the baby and experienced a sharp longing so severe she had to grip the edge of the crib for support.

"But?"

She swallowed hard and stared at Rebecca. "But my career—"

"Comes first? Yeah—I got that, Grace."

"No one gets both," she said quietly, suddenly numb.

He didn't say anything. The tension coursing through him was palpable and vibrated around the room. Grace longed to touch him, to reach for his face and hold him between her shaking hands. It had been so long since they'd touched and her skin ached with the need to feel the heat of his body. But she didn't move. Didn't dare ask him to take her in his arms.

*What if we never touch again?*

"In your world...I guess not," he said quietly.

The door opened and Evie walked back into the room. She hesitated for a moment, clearly sensing the tension in the room, and then plastered on a big smile.

"How's my girl?" she asked cheerfully and walked across to the crib. "Did she miss me?"

Grace pulled her composure together. "She's been a perfect angel." She touched Rebecca's tiny head for a moment before she grabbed her handbag. "I'll head off." She hugged her sister close, hanging on for as long as she could, feeling Evie's innate strength and unquestioning love. "I'll see you soon."

Evie nodded. "Sure."

She didn't look at Cameron. If he saw her eyes, if he were to look deep within her he'd know she was on the brink of a meltdown. She took a gulp of air, said goodbye to her sister and muttered another in his direction and left the room. And she didn't take another breath until she was halfway down the corridor.

Evie Jones's stare made it clear to Cameron that he was in for an earful. He tried to ignore it. "Your daughter is beautiful, Evie," he said and stepped around the mobile crib. "No doubt Scott is—"

"Can I ask you something?" she queried, cutting him off, hands firmly on hips.

He took a second to respond. "Ah—okay."

"Are you really in love with my sister?" she asked bluntly.

He stilled. "Well, I—"

"Because if you are," she said, cutting him off again, "you've a strange way of showing it."

Cameron had always liked Evie. But he wasn't about to get into a conversation about his feelings for her sister. Even if he understood Evie's motives and natural loyalty toward Grace. "She's made her choice."

Evie harrumphed. "Looks like you have, too," she said with bite. "To act like a jerk, I mean."

Why was it that all the women around him seemed to be dishing out insults and advice? First his mother, now Evie. "What did Grace tell you?"

"Enough," Evie replied. "And I know my sister. Better than you do, by the looks of things."

Cameron reined in the irritation weaving up his spine. "I know she wants her career more than...more than anything else."

"Rubbish," Evie scolded, not holding back. "What she wants—what she's always wanted, probably even before she knew it herself—is you."

It was exactly what he wanted to hear. But Cameron wasn't about to get sucked in by Evie's romantic notions. "I know you're trying to help, but—"

"What I'm trying to do," she said, making no attempt to stop interrupting him, "—is understand why you've given up on her so easily."

That got his attention. "And what exactly do you suggest I do, beg her to stay?"

Evie blew out a weary breath and looked at him intently. "If that's what it takes."

Cameron swallowed hard. "I can't do that."

"Even if it means you could lose her forever?"

*I've already lost her.* It was a ridiculous conversation. "I thought I'd done enough when I asked her to marry me."

"She's scared of...feelings," Evie said with a sigh.

"I know she is," he said and pushed back the pain behind his ribs. "But I can't do any more."

Evie didn't look surprised by his words. "Can't? Or won't?"

"She made her choice."

"I see. So this is about pride?" Evie asked.

Heat rushed through his blood. "It's about knowing when I'm beat."

She'd rejected him again and he wasn't about to go back for another dose. Not now. Not ever.

## Chapter Thirteen

New York greeted her with same bright lights and never-ending energy that she remembered.

Grace holed up in her apartment for three days before she pulled herself together, dressed in her best power suit and hightailed it back to her office. Her assistant had a stack of emails, files and interoffice memos waiting for her. There was enough work to keep her busy for the next two months, including weekends.

*At least I won't have time to think about anything else.*

Or anyone.

*Or someone.*

She pushed herself all day and when her boss came into her office around four carrying two foam cups of coffee, Grace closed down her laptop and stretched her shoulders.

"So, how was the vacation?" Jennifer Mullin-Shaw asked as she passed her the coffee.

Grace had worked for Shapiro, Cross & Shaw for eight

years. Jennifer had been made partner fifteen years earlier and was the epitome of a committed, successful career woman. For many years Grace had wanted to emulate the other woman. She wanted to be a partner one day. She wanted the money and prestige and to be respected among her peers the way Jennifer was. A couple more years and she knew she'd get there.

"It was fine," she said and drank some coffee.

"And you're feeling better?"

"Fine."

Jennifer, always business, nodded. "So, you're fine? Ready to get back to work?"

Grace pointed to the computer. "I've enough to keep me busy for the next few months."

Jennifer sank into the chair opposite her and looked over the rim of her cup. "There's a spot opening up. Kurt's moving to Chicago. Better salary, bigger office. Interested?"

Grace straightened. Five weeks ago she wouldn't have hesitated to say yes. Five weeks ago she wanted the bigger office and better salary.

Five weeks ago she wasn't prepared to admit she was hopelessly in love with Cameron Jakowski.

"Of course," she said with as much enthusiasm as she could muster.

"It means more high-profile clients," Jennifer said as both brows came up. "Which equates to longer hours and pretty much means you can say goodbye to your personal life. Are you ready for that?"

"Sure."

Jennifer nodded and stood. "Good. I'll talk to Jim and Harris," she said of the two other partners in the firm. "And we'll make it official next week. Congratulations, you've earned this."

Grace got to her feet. "Thank you."

The other woman headed for the door, but turned before she crossed the threshold. "Are you sure you're okay, Grace? You seem distracted."

"I'm fine," she assured her. "Just a little jet-lagged."

"Well, I'm pleased the vacation did the trick for you. It's good to have you back."

As she watched Jennifer disappear her insides were strangely empty.

Grace could barely believe it. A promotion. A new office. She'd arrived at the pinnacle of her chosen profession. It was everything she'd worked toward. *I'm back. I made it.* She should have been jumping through hoops.

Instead, she had a hollow spot in the middle of her chest that seemed to be getting deeper and deeper each day. Five weeks ago she'd returned to Crystal Point, broken and afraid. Miraculously, she'd healed those wounds and made peace with her guilt and fear. Life moved on. *She'd* moved on.

And still the hollowness prevailed, settling behind her ribs, making her remember how she got to be standing alone in her office. And what she'd left behind. In the window Grace caught her own reflection. The black suit, killer heels, perfectly straight hair. All she saw was a stranger, a facsimile of a woman she'd once been.

*I have the career I've always wanted. I have the life I've always wanted. It's here, for me to take.*

And yet…another life now beckoned. A life she missed. And suddenly she longed to be that woman again. The woman who'd felt like she was really part of her family for the first time. The woman who'd helped Emily ace her makeup exam and who'd spent a crazy weekend with Pat Jennings and her adorable grandchildren. The woman who'd left her hair to create its own curly madness and loped around in paint-stained clothes. And the woman who'd experienced such an acute connection with Cameron she could barely draw breath without remembering how it felt to lie in his arms.

She'd been so determined to not feel anything and to not be derailed, but as she looked out the window, Grace knew she was the world's biggest hypocrite. Because she'd told Emily it *was* possible to have it all. In that last week during their tutoring sessions she'd spouted speeches about having both a career and a family. A career and a personal life.

*Do as I say, not as I do.*

Memories bombarded her. Bathing the twins. Sharing tea with her mother. Jed loping beside her. Emily looking so proud of her achievements. Holding Evie's baby. And Cameron.

*The man I love.*

The man she'd always loved. Even at eighteen. Or sixteen, when he'd kissed her for the first time. And through the years where their relationship had been fraught with insults and goading and so much simmering tension.

*And he's in love with me, too.*

The city below made noises she couldn't hear from the lonely spot in her ivory tower. And as if a great wave of peace had washed over her, Grace knew exactly what she wanted.

She packed the laptop into her case and flung it over her shoulder, grabbed her handbag and jacket and left the room. A few minutes later she tapped on Jennifer's office door and was quickly beckoned inside.

"Grace?" The other woman looked at her bags and jacket. "You're heading off?"

She took a deep breath and a smile curved her mouth. "Actually…I'm going home."

"I can't believe I passed that exam."

Emily's excitement was great to see and Cameron nodded. "I told you that you would."

"I know," she said, and shrugged. "You and Nan both believed I could do it. And Grace."

His back stiffened. It was hard to hear her name. Harder still to not think about her twenty-four hours a day. "Just keep hitting the books and you'll get a good final grade."

"Good enough to go to night school I hope," Emily said cheerfully and bounced Riley on her knee. "Grace made some inquiries for me when she was here."

"She's special, that one," Pat said from her spot at the table and looked directly at him. "But I guess you know that already."

Cameron had dropped Dylan home after the Big Brother meeting and stayed for coffee. He hadn't planned on every part of the conversation being about Grace. "I've organized the moving truck for next Tuesday," he told Emily, ignoring Pat's question as politely as he could.

"Great," the teenager said. "I can't wait to get my own place." She quickly patted her grandmother's hand. "Not that I don't like living here with everyone, because I do. But it will be awesome for Riley to have his own room. And once I get my driver's license I can come and see you all in Burdon Creek every few weeks."

It was a good plan, and one he'd help see through to fruition. They were a strong family, despite the challenges they'd faced, and Cameron knew they'd be okay.

"You know," Pat said and stirred her tea. "I hear New York's quite the place to visit."

He didn't miss the point. "I'm not much for big cities."

No, he was small town. Grace was big city. Oil and water. He should have known better, right? In some ways he knew he'd been waiting for her rejection since that night on the beach. And she hadn't disappointed. His pride took another battering. So he'd bailed.

In every other part of his life, in every other part of himself, Cameron was rational and reasonable. He forgave, he compromised, and he fought for what he believed in. But this was different. Because he'd told Grace he loved her and she hadn't said the same. She hadn't admitted anything. She'd made him hurt and he felt that hurt through to the marrow in his bones. It was excruciating, soul destroying. He was a small-town police officer and that wasn't enough.

His love wasn't enough.

*He* wasn't enough.

Just like he hadn't been for his father.

Cameron's breath suddenly twisted like a knot in his chest. Damn. There it was—the real reason he'd let her go without a fight. In a way it was the same reason he worked so hard to be a good man…to prove his worth. To override the loss of the father who hadn't wanted him. That's why Grace's rejection when they were young had affected him so deeply. Because he'd felt like he wasn't worthy, like he wasn't enough to have her love. Then resentment and dislike had kicked in and he'd spent the next fifteen years behaving like an incomparable ass.

Until she'd come back and he'd realized that he still loved her, still wanted her, and more. He needed her. Like the air he breathed. Like water he drank. Grace was in his blood, his heart, his soul. And he missed her perfectly beautiful face.

But what could he do? Pat's idea was out of the question. He wasn't about to hightail it to New York to face the blunt force of another rejection—no matter how much he wanted to see her.

Only a crazy man would do that, right?

Grace was back in Crystal Point. It was late Sunday afternoon when she pulled her rental car outside her parent's home. There were several other cars out front, including the familiar sight of Cameron's electric-blue Ford sedan. She knew from Evie that her mother had organized a party to celebrate Rebecca's arrival.

*I can do this,* she thought as she headed through the front door.

She heard the party coming from the back patio area and made her way down the hall. Grace found her mother in the kitchen and dropped her bag on the counter.

Barbara swiveled around instantly. "Grace!" she exclaimed, quickly looking her over, clearly taking in Grace's disheveled appearance as she came around the counter. "What are you doing here? Are you okay?"

Grace accepted her mother's warm embrace and held on. When she pulled back the other woman's expression was one of deep concern. "I've been so foolish. And so blind."

Barbara frowned slightly. "What do you mean?"

Before she could reply heels clicked over tiles and they both stepped back. Irene Jakowski walked into the kitchen and came to a stunned halt. "Grace...you're here?"

Grace swallowed a lump in her throat. "Yes," she whispered.

Irene smiled warmly. "Good girl."

She managed a smile and her breath came out as a shudder when she looked toward the doors that led outside. "Is... is he..."

Irene nodded and squeezed her arm. "He is."

She took a few steps forward. "Thank you."

Barbara Preston watched her daughter walk outside and turned to her best friend. "What was that all about? What does it mean?"

Irene grinned broadly. "I think it means that one day you and I will probably be sharing grandchildren."

Cameron had walked through the family room and onto the back patio when he heard someone call Grace's name.

Stupid. He heard her name everywhere. On the street. On the television. In his dreams.

But this caught his attention. He stopped in the doorway and looked around.

And there she stood.

Like a vision. A beautiful vision with her hair curling wildly around her face. She wore jeans and an old shirt. *His* shirt he realized after a microsecond. *She's wearing my shirt. She's here and she's wearing my shirt.* His heart almost burst through his chest.

The dozen or so people on the patio all stilled. And stared. She stared back, from one to the next. And then she found him with her gaze. In that moment no one else existed and his mind soared with a hazy kind of hope. He fought the urge to go to her, staying back, head spinning.

*She's here.*

Cameron's gaze flicked to the group of curious people watching her…taking in her hair and clothes and the faintly expectant expression on her face. She did look different than the Grace they were used to. They were used to the usual perfection of her immaculate clothing and straight hair. Funny, but she always seemed perfect to him. His mind was bombarded with memories—Grace in the morning, her hair spread out on his pillow. A sleepy Grace who couldn't keep her eyes open as they watched television together. Grace coming apart in his arms when they made love.

"Can I…can I talk to you?" she asked hesitantly, looking only at him.

The twenty feet between them suddenly seemed like a huge divide—especially with their respective families watching on the sidelines. Maybe he should have suggested they go inside. But he didn't want to move…he didn't want to shift the incredible contact throbbing between them.

"Okay…talk."

Her eyes widened and glittered. She wouldn't do this in front of her family. Or would she? He tried to be cool and rested one shoulder against the doorjamb and watched as she swallowed hard.

"Here?"

Cameron nodded. "Here."

She glanced at the sea of curious faces watching their exchange and shook her head fractionally. Cameron looked across the patio and saw Evie nodding, almost prompting her sister to continue. He watched and panic rose when she stepped back. She turned on her heels and walked toward the door to the house. His mother was there. As was Barbara Preston.

After a moment she turned again, back to him. Relief pitched in his chest when he saw strength in her eyes.

"You were right," she said quietly and crossed her arms over his paint-splattered shirt. "About me. About everything."

Cameron waited, breathless.

"I *have* always wanted to be perfect," she stressed, looking at him. "But after the accident I was so far from that. I was out of control. I felt weak, like I'd lost my edge. It was as if I'd been cut off at the knees."

"And?" he asked, trying to appear casual even though his insides were jumping all over the place.

"And I came back here to refocus. I had to prove that I could be that person again—the one who was ambitious and strong and successful—because that's who I'd been raised to be. That's what defined me. I knew I had to take back my life and not be afraid, and not feel so wretchedly guilty that I'd survived and someone else had died." She drew in a deep breath. "So, I *did* refocus. Then I went back to New York and got a promotion the very day I returned to work." She drew in another breath, shakier, short. "And it would have been a great job."

Cameron straightened and pushed himself off the door. *"Would have?"*

She nodded. "I quit."

More gasps echoed around the patio. Cameron could barely get his words out. "You quit? Why?"

He saw her lip tremble and watched, both fascinated and agonized as her green eyes filled with tears.

"Because I didn't want to make the biggest mistake of my life." Her voice quivered, almost breaking. "So, I quit, like I said. Which means I'm unemployed." She raised her shoulders and dropped them heavily. "I've decided I'm going to work for myself now. Freelance. I'll get a few clients and who knows…" She blinked at the wetness threatening to fall. "All I know is that I can do that anywhere. I can do that…here."

Cameron harnessed his feelings. They weren't done yet. He had to know more. He had to know how she really felt. "And will that be enough?" *Will I be enough? Will we be enough?*

Grace nodded. "I've been incredibly stupid. And afraid. And dishonest with myself. And with you," she added. "I want things. I want all those things we talked about. I do want my career…but I want everything else, too. I want a home and a family and…and who says a person can't have b-both?" She hiccupped and clasped her arms tightly around herself.

"I guess it depends how much you want them."

She nodded. "I want them badly enough to stand here and make a complete fool out of myself right now."

Cameron bit back a grin. She *was* making a fool of herself. A beautiful, perfectly adorable fool. "And you're doing that because?"

Grace drew in a breath and glanced at the stunned, silent people standing on the edge of the patio. Emotion choked her eyes, her heart and her skin. They were her family and she wasn't being judged as weak or foolish or any of the things she'd always feared.

"Because…" she said shakily and let the tears come, over her lids and down her cheeks. "Because when I'm with you I'm the best version of myself. And I'm…just…so much in love with you."

There it was. Her heart laid out for everyone to see. She ignored the shocked gasps from the sidelines. Ignored everything and everyone except Cameron.

He hadn't moved. But he looked deep into her eyes. Into that place made only for him. Grace tried to smile, hoping to see love and acceptance and forgiveness.

"Say something," she whispered.

He grinned. "You're wearing my shirt."

Grace unhooked her arms and touched the fabric. "It was all I had of you."

"It's not all you have, Grace." He smiled broadly and she saw the love in his expression. "Whatever I am, with every part of who I am…you've always had every bit of my heart."

Relief and love and gratitude flowed through her and she kept crying, but they were happy tears she was proud to show. "So, will you ask me that question again? Because if you do, I'll promise to get the answer right this time."

He laughed softly and looked toward the people staring at them, all stunned by what they had heard. Except Evie, who was smiling the biggest smile and holding her baby against her chest. And Irene Jakowski, who looked at Grace as though she had just hung the moon.

He nodded. "I'm asking."

Grace laughed, happiness radiating through her. "And I'm saying yes."

His smile reached right into her heart. "Then get over here," he beckoned softly.

She took about two seconds before she raced across the patio and flung herself into his arms. For the first time in her life she didn't give a hoot what anyone thought of her. She didn't care that some of her family were now looking at her as though she'd lost her mind. Serious, overachieving, humorless Grace was gone. She didn't want to be *perfect*. She simply wanted to love this incredible man who'd somehow managed to love her too despite her prickly, icy reserve.

He kissed her then, right there, in front of the world, and Grace gave up her heart, her soul, her very self, and kissed him back.

"Am I the only one who didn't know about this?" Grace heard Noah ask in an incredulous voice. She also heard Callie's "no, dear," and smiled beneath the pressure of Cameron's kiss.

Finally they pulled apart. He smiled and gazed down at her. "Let's get out of here," he suggested and grasped her hand. "So I can do this properly."

Grace took a deep breath and vaguely heard him excuse them both. Within less than a minute they were inside the house and he pulled her down onto the sofa in the living room.

"I don't think poor Noah is over the shock," she said, laughing.

Cameron molded her shoulders with his hands and looked into her eyes. "He'll get used to the idea," he assured her. "Once we're married."

"Married?" she echoed dreamily.

He looked panicky all of a sudden. "You did agree to marry me, didn't you?"

She nodded. "Yes. But you'll need this to make it official," she said and pulled the ring he'd offered her weeks ago from her pocket. "It really is beautiful."

"You kept it?"

She nodded. "Of course I did. I've been carrying it with me everywhere."

"Does it fit?" he asked and took the ring from her fingertips.

Grace shrugged. "I'm not sure. I didn't dare try it on. I wanted to…so much."

Cameron smiled deeply and grabbed her left hand. "Where it belongs," he said as he easily slipped the ring onto her finger. "Now and forever, Princess."

Grace's heart did a flip. Hearing him call her Princess was the most wonderful thing she'd ever heard. "I'm so sorry, Cameron. For every time I made you feel like I didn't want this…that I didn't want *us*. I'm sorry for being the foolish girl I was at eighteen who didn't have the sense to see what was right in front her. And I'm sorry for being so self-centered that I—"

"Grace, I—"

"Let me finish," she said and placed a gentle finger against his mouth. She moved her hand to his cheek and held him there. "You are, without a doubt, the most amazing man I have ever known. You're strong and honest and honorable and so incredibly kind. To love you…to be loved by you… is truly humbling."

"That's very sweet, Grace," he said and kissed her softly.

"I'm not sweet at all," she defied as their lips parted. "And you know it. In fact, you probably know me better than anyone."

"I know you're in my heart, Grace. I know I love you more than I ever imagined I could love anyone."

"I love you, too," she said and experienced a swell of love so deep, and so rich, it tore the breath from her throat. "For so long I've been afraid to truly feel anything. I had my career and let that define me…I let that be all that I was. But I was hollow inside." She gripped his hands. "You saved me," she said quietly. "You saved me when I came back and didn't know how tell my family about the accident. You saved me by letting me tutor Emily, which showed me how good it feels to really do something for someone else. And you saved me every time you held me and made me feel less broken. When I think of how close I came to making the wrong choice…" She shuddered.

He brought her hands to his lips and kissed them softly. "You're here now. We're here now. That's all that matters."

"But I—"

"No buts," he insisted and smiled. "Although now is probably a good time to talk about the flight I just booked to New York."

Grace's eyes filled with more tears. "You…you were coming to see me?"

He smiled warmly. "Of course. To see you—or to bring you back—or live there with you. Either way, Grace, being apart from you was never an option."

"But you didn't say anything like that before."

"I'm an idiot," he said flatly. "And too proud to admit I was afraid of rejection. You knew that," he said as he touched her face. "You asked me why I help kids like Dylan and I wasn't honest with you. I don't think I really understood why until the other day. All my life I've felt like I had to somehow make up for my biological father running out on me and my mother, as though in some way it would make the hurt go away." He clutched her hands and his voice broke with emotion as he said the words. "And it stopped me from being truly grateful for the father I have."

"You do have a good father," she assured him.

He kissed her softly. "I know. And, Grace, if you want to go to back to New York, if you want that promotion, then we'll go—together. And if you want to stay in Crystal Point, we'll stay."

Grace closed her eyes for a moment. When she opened them again he was watching her with blistering intensity. "I want to stay," she replied. "I want to marry you and live in your house. I want us to take Jed for long walks along the beach. I want to share our life with our families. I want to be at your side in this community and help kids like Dylan and Emily. And one day soon, I want to have your baby."

He raised a brow. "You want kids? You really do?"

What she wanted had never seemed clearer. "I really do."

He kissed her. Long and sweet and filled with love. "I love you, Grace, so much."

She smiled, remembering what Pat had said to her.

*There's a lot to be said about the love of a good man.*

Yes, Grace thought as she pressed against him, there certainly was.

* * * * *

Look out for
**Mills & Boon® TEMPTED™ 2-in-1s,**
from September

*Fresh, contemporary romances
to tempt all lovers of
great stories*

*A sneaky peek at next month…*

# Cherish™

**ROMANCE TO MELT THE HEART EVERY TIME**

## *My wish list for next month's titles…*

In stores from 16th August 2013:

☐ A Marriage Made in Italy – Rebecca Winters

& The Cowboy She Couldn't Forget – Patricia Thayer

☐ Miracle in Bellaroo Creek – Barbara Hannay

& Patchwork Family in the Outback – Soraya Lane

In stores from 6th September 2013:

☐ The Maverick & the Manhattanite – Leanne Banks

& A Very Special Delivery – Brenda Harlen

☐ The Courage To Say Yes – Barbara Wallace

& Her McKnight in Shining Armour – Teresa Southwick

Available at WHSmith, Tesco, Asda, Eason, Amazon and Apple

## *Just can't wait?*

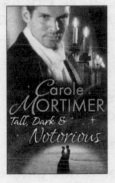
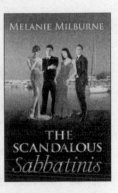

# MILLS & BOON®
## *Book Club*

# *Join the Mills & Boon Book Club*

---

Want to read more **Cherish**™ books?
We're offering you **2 more** absolutely **FREE!**

---

We'll also treat you to these fabulous extras:

- **Exclusive offers and much more!**

- **FREE home delivery**

- **FREE books and gifts with our special rewards scheme**

*Get your free books now!*

## visit www.millsandboon.co.uk/bookclub
## or call Customer Relations on 020 8288 2888